Year of the Tiger

Alison Lloyd

Holiday House / New York

For the Lord of all history
And my family

Text copyright © Alison Lloyd, 2008
First published in 2008 by Penguin Group (Australia),
a division of Pearson Australia Group, Ltd.

The moral right of the author has been asserted.

First published in the United States of America by Holiday House in 2010
HOLIDAY HOUSE is registered in the U.S. Patent and Trademark Office.
Printed in the United States of America
www.holidayhouse.com
First American Edition
1   3   5   7   9   10   8   6   4   2

Library of Congress Cataloging-in-Publication Data

Lloyd, Alison, 1966-
Year of the tiger / by Alison Lloyd.—1 st American ed.
p. cm.
Summary: In ancient China, two boys forge an unlikely alliance in an effort to become
expert archers and, ultimately, to save their city from invading barbarians.
ISBN 978-0-8234-2277-7 (hardcover)
[1. Archery—Fiction.   2. Social classes—Fiction.   3. Adventure and
adventurers—Fiction.   4. China—History—Han dynasty,
202 B.C.-220 A.D.—Fiction.]   I. Title.
PZ7.L77876Ye 2010
[Fic]—dc22
2009033651

Chinese names and words in *Year of the Tiger*

Ah-po	*(Pronounced "Ah-poor")*	Grandma (mother's mother)
Beicheng	*("Bay-cherng")*	Imaginary place in northwest China; meaning "North Town"
Ding	*(Rhymes with "ring")*	The Magistrate of Beicheng; surname, meaning "man" or "nail"
Han	*("Hahn")*	Name for a dynasty, or series of emperors, who ruled China from 207 BC to AD 220; Chinese people today still use this name for themselves and their language
Hu	*("Who")*	Meaning "tiger"
kang	*("Kahng")*	Hollow brick platform used as a bed and a stove; heated in winter
Li	*("Lee")*	Hu's surname
Li San	*("Lee Sahn")*	Hu's father; meaning "Li Three," the third son of his family
Lien	*("Lee-en")*	Ren's sister; meaning "compassion"
Luoyang	*("Law-young")*	Capital of China in the Eastern Han dynasty, AD 25–190
Ma	*("Mah")*	Mom

Mei	*("May")*	Hu's sister; meaning "plum blossom"
Ren	*("Rern")*	Meaning "benevolence, kindness"
Wang	*(Rhymes with "sung")*	Ren's tutor; a common surname
Wuzhong	*("Woo-joong")*	A town on the Yellow River in northern China
Zheng	*("Jerng")*	Ren's surname

In Chinese, people put their surnames in front of their first names. So the main characters of this book are Li Hu and Zheng Ren. It is friendly and polite to call people by their titles, such as "Second Deputy" (or "Number Two" for those who know him well).

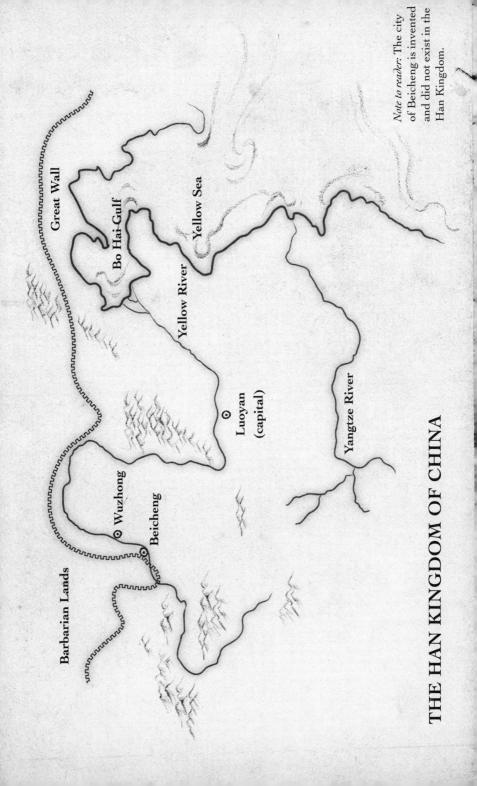

THE HAN KINGDOM OF CHINA

Great Wall

Bo Hai Gulf

Yellow Sea

Yellow River

Luoyan
(capital)

Yangtze River

Wuzhong

Beicheng

Barbarian Lands

Note to reader: The city
of Beicheng is invented
and did not exist in the
Han Kingdom.

PROLOGUE
The First Half of the Tiger Goes Out

From His Imperial Majesty,
Ruler of the Han Kingdom,
To honorable Commander Zheng,
Tiger Battalion,

You are hereby instructed
to lead your battalion to Beicheng,
on our northern border. You are authorized
to conduct inspections and repairs of the Great Wall.

I, the Emperor, charge you with this duty:
strengthen our defenses;
preserve the peace and prosperity of the Kingdom.

No military action or contact
with the barbarians is permitted.

By Imperial Order,
Tenth Year of the Reign

夏

SUMMER

HU

"Legendary archer Yi fits an arrow to his bow and draws. The string thrums. . . ." Li Hu sent a stick arrow flying from his home-made bow. "Bull's-eye!"

It went straight through the loop in his sister's hair and out over the battlements.

Hu and Mei were on top of the Great Wall. In front of them was China: the Han Kingdom. Behind them were the outside lands, roamed by barbarians and evil spirits. The Wall stretched to either side for ten thousand miles, as tall as four men, keeping the barbarians out. At least it was sup-posed to, but the section of Wall beside Hu and Mei had long ago collapsed into a weedy heap of rubble.

"*Ai*—there's not much call for legendary archers around here," said Mei, crumbling a piece off the watchtower. She looked sideways at Hu and then spoke gently. "Nobody's told you this, because they know you won't like it. But today—"

"Mei! Did you see that?"

Hu was not interested in bad news. A sudden movement had caught his eye—a flash of gold in the green bushes, near the base of the tower.

"*Mmm?* What?"

"A tiger!"

"You've got too much imagination. There aren't any tigers around here, except you, and you're pretty tame," Mei said. Hu was born in the year of the Tiger. Mei was two years older.

"Am not, you Rat! It's the year of the Tiger again, and Ah-po says I'm going to meet my destiny soon." Ah-po was their grandmother.

"Well, watch out it doesn't gobble you up," said Mei.

Hu was annoyed. He didn't want Mei to be gloomy. He didn't want to be reminded of the fears lurking in the back of his mind.

"Why do you have to be so boring?" he said.

"I'm not boring, just practical. Poor people have it tough. You have to expect that, or you'll be disappointed."

"That's weak," said Hu. But he knew she was right—things could get worse. Last year, a boy had turned up in the town marketplace so thin his cheeks stood out like knuckles. He had nothing except a broken bowl for begging. He disappeared, but the memory of him stuck with Hu. He wanted to be full and safe.

The Li family ran a noodle stall, and it got them pretty well nowhere, despite the hard slog. Every day, he and Mei lugged firewood downhill and water uphill. They still had hardly any food and no money. Hu wanted to do something better. His family should have been able to make a living as singers and acrobats, and Hu loved acting out the old stories of mighty warriors. But Magistrate Ding, who was in charge of the district, was tight as a closed fist with his cash. He hadn't asked the Lis to do a show in ages, and he was the one who paid.

Mei picked up the empty buckets. "Don't forget—we still have to go get water."

In the valley below, their hometown of Beicheng perched above the Yellow River. From Beicheng the river snaked away to the far-distant capital, like coil after coil of a giant golden dragon. Shame the river wasn't really made of gold—it was just yellow dirt, like everything else around Beicheng.

"You see that?" Mei said, pointing.

On the road by the river, a lone man was walking slowly away from town. He was bent under the weight of a basket on his back.

"Know who that is?" she demanded.

Hu looked harder. He did know. It was their father, Li San.

"What?" he said. "Is that our basket?" His stomach growled with doubt and hunger.

"I think so," said Mei. "He's going to sell the costumes and the props. I was trying to tell you that before."

"But how can we perform without them?" Hu said. This was bad. Without the performing props, they were one step closer to having nothing at all.

"We've got to stop him," he yelled to Mei. He shoved his makeshift bow back into his pile of sticks and hauled the load of firewood down the steps of the watchtower.

He struggled through the sloping grain fields toward the road. Mei followed, calling out to him to slow down. Buckets and sticks banged against their legs as they hurried and sweated in the midday sun.

Suddenly, out of the shimmering heat, a fabulous, glittering sight appeared. . . .

REN

The procession wound around a corner of the road to Beicheng. Hundreds of horses, soldiers, carts, and chariots kicked up clouds of yellow dust. Carrying the Tiger Battalion's banner at the front was an officer in bronze-studded leather armor, with a scar across his jaw. Riding behind his First Deputy, on a magnificent white horse, the Commander of the battalion scanned the surroundings.

The procession was passing through a gorge. The river was narrow, and the road carved into the cliff face. From his seat in an open carriage, the Commander's son, Ren, peered over the edge. Yellow water ran fast and dirty at the bottom of a sheer drop. Ren's little sister, Lien, whimpered and clung to him with hot, sticky hands. Ren shook her off.

"Be a nasty place for a fight, wouldn't it?" the Second Deputy said to Ren, steering the carriage horses away from the road's edge.

"Who are we going to fight out here?" asked Ren eagerly.

"Nobody," said Second Deputy. "We're here to fix the Wall so we won't have to fight." He flicked dirt off his high, varnished boots. "Reach behind your sister, if you please, Young Master Zheng, and get the map. I'll show you something."

Ren was pleased. His father's Second Deputy, a real officer, was talking to him like an equal. He had called him Young

Master. Back home in the capital, a month's journey behind them, his father's First Wife would never have allowed that. Only her sons, his half brothers, were given such attention in the house she controlled.

This was the first time Ren had come out on an expedition with his father and the battalion. Since his mother had died two years ago, Ren had learned to be tough. He didn't cry when his half brothers picked on him, not like Lien did.

He had swelled with pride when the Commander had decided to bring him on the Emperor's mission. Here was his chance, Ren thought, to show his father who he was, to show him that his youngest son could make a good nobleman, maybe even a Commander one day.

He pulled the map case from under his sister and unrolled the scroll across his knees. The Great Wall ran in zigzag brushstrokes across the top of the silk square, almost the whole length of China's north.

"This dot here is where we're going." Second Deputy pointed with the handle of his whip. "It's called Beicheng. See how it's positioned between the Wall and this narrow bit of river? After that it's a clean sweep from here across the plains to the capital. That's why the Wall and the town are here. To stop the barbarian tribes before they loot and burn their way right to the Emperor's doorstep."

"Why don't we attack them first?" Ren asked.

"Ah. We've got orders not to. That would break the deal the Emperor's agreed to. If you ask me," said Second Deputy, leaning conspiratorially toward Ren, "the Emperor is rather trusting of his savage friends. He's signed a peace treaty with their chief, and he thinks it's going to hold."

In front, Commander Zheng abruptly reined in his horse

and turned around. He was frowning; his jagged eyebrows were like two bolts of black lightning.

"But the boy didn't ask you," he said. "He will follow orders and not ask questions. As you know, Number Two, obedience pleases both Heaven and the Emperor."

It didn't please Ren, however. He wanted to know a lot more. He wanted to be included in everything.

He looked at Second Deputy, but the officer was steering the horses around a tight bend. Around the corner, the road opened into a valley full of grain fields. The millet was knee-high and full of singing cicadas but little else. It didn't look much like a battlefield to Ren.

A man was coming the other way, loaded with a basket. He looked up at the approaching battalion. His mouth dropped open in surprise, and he hurried off the road to let them pass.

All of a sudden the horses shied and tossed their heads. The carriage lurched, and Lien fell across Ren's lap. But it was only a couple of scruffy peasant children leaping through the grain field toward them. A boy and an older girl, gaping at the army going past.

They should admire us, thought Ren. His world was way above theirs.

As they got closer to Beicheng, Second Deputy smoothed his hair with one hand and flicked more dust off his boots.

"Can you teach me to drive a chariot?" Ren asked. He knew a bit about horses, and he was itching to hold the reins.

"You'll have to ask your father," the officer replied with a wink.

They rolled up toward the dusty town, followed by the marching troops. The peasant and the children came after the soldiers, walking a respectful distance behind.

HU

The day after the army's arrival, Li San was summoned up to see Magistrate Ding.

"It'll be taxes or trouble or both," said Ma. She punched the ball of noodle dough and dumped the water pot on the *kang* to heat.

Hu pinched off a piece of dough and ate it while her back was turned. Then he pinched the dough some more until it had two eyes, a big nose, and a little beard like the Magistrate.

"There," he said to his mother. "Go for him!" Hu wanted her to smile. He didn't like people being worried all the time. But even he had wondered all day what the army's coming meant. No one from the capital had ever come to Beicheng before, not for as long as he could remember. The capital was as far away as the mountain of the Immortals.

Li San returned, grinning. He ducked under the low door, clapped Hu over the shoulder, and reached for the bronze gong hanging on the wall.

"Old Hard-as-Nails is finally being forced to hand out some cash," he said. "Nail" was the meaning of Magistrate Ding's surname, so Hard-as-Nails was one of the names he got called behind his back.

"*Aiya*," said Ah-po, Hu's grandmother. "Such disrespect."

Hu laughed. He loved it when his father made fun of important people.

Li San rapped the gong with his knuckles. It rang with a low tremor.

"Tomorrow . . ." he announced with a dramatic pause, "there's a banquet to welcome the military big shots. Our worthy Magistrate Ding is the host. The guest of honor is one Commander Zheng, of the Imperial Army." Li San bowed low. "And *we*, the lucky Lis, are performing in the town hall!"

Hu whooped and Mei cheered. They would be paid! Maybe the army would turn his family's fortunes around.

"So," Li San went on, "we check all the props and costumes. Just as well I didn't get far with them, eh?"

"Although Hu's costume pants will be above his knees by now," Ma said.

"Well, we've got to put in our best effort ever. Nothing slapdash. We have to be as good as the Monkey King himself." Li San tapped the gong again and struck a Monkey King pose. "Or the Magistrate will lose face, we'll lose face, and we'll never get another performance, sure as beggars go hungry. Do you understand?"

Hu and Mei nodded.

Their father dropped his voice and spoke to Ma. "The Magistrate wants to sweeten them up, I'm guessing. The rumor is they've come to look at the Wall."

"Will they want to look at this bit?" asked Hu, cocking his head toward the back of the room. The Lis' home was built right up against the town wall, near the marketplace and the main south gates.

"Not the town wall, featherhead—the Great Wall," Mei told Hu. "Noble people don't come to the bottom end of town."

Hu pulled a face. On the other side of the town wall, exactly next to their room, was a compost heap where the market's scraps were dumped. Next to that was the public toilet, where other things got dumped. In summer, the stink rose with the heat. "High smells, low rent," Ma retorted if Hu complained.

Hu's imagination was doing somersaults at the thought of putting on a show for the Commander and his army.

"What'll we perform?" he asked Li San.

Hu's father handed him the gong and lifted the lid of the large basket in the corner. He took out a wooden bow. It had been a real soldier's weapon once. Now it was painted in bright colors, like the flags of the army. Hu's father bent it carefully around his knee and hooked the bowstring over one end.

"We'll do *The Legend of Archer Yi*—it's good for soldiers," he answered.

"Yes!" said Hu.

Ma clapped her hands, showering everyone with flour. "We can get credit at the grain store again," she said.

Hu and Mei were sent off with careful instructions about what flour to get at what price from the grain store.

"Let's go past the town hall," Hu said to Mei after they'd bought a sackful and loaded it in their wheelbarrow. The grain store was near the town hall, which had been taken over by the battalion. Hu wanted to have a look.

"We're supposed to go straight home," Mei said.

Hu rolled his eyes. "Come on!"

Even before they got to the hall, Hu and Mei saw a new banner on top of the tower. It was red, embroidered with big green characters, and it had gold tassels that caught the sunlight. Hoof marks led straight through the hall's gates into the courtyard. Hu pushed the wheelbarrow into the shade of the gate to have a look inside.

"*Wei!*" A yell came from the guard by the gate. He was a big man with a long spear in one hand and a green band along the flap of his jacket. He pushed himself off the wall and sauntered forward. He had big ears that stuck out like cabbage leaves.

"No peasant puppies allowed here. This is Imperial headquarters. Shove off!"

Hu could barely understand the soldier's hissing southern accent.

Hu and Mei didn't move fast enough for the guard's liking. The man frowned and shook his spear to shoo them away. "*Ya! Ya!*"

"Hold on a minute." Another green-banded soldier, a smaller man, came from the other side of the gateway. He smiled; he had yellow teeth that poked forward like a rat's.

"What brings you here, sweetie?" he asked Mei. He had an accent too, but he spoke to her slowly, like someone coaxing a shy animal. "Come by for a visit? Nice to have a bit of company, seeing as how we can't leave our post, eh?" He cast a glance toward the other soldier, who shuffled his big feet nervously.

Hu looked at his sister, who bowed her head. She could be sweet as honey on the outside, but she usually knew a lot more than she let on. Ma said she was smart and sent her to deal with the grain merchant and difficult customers. But soldiers were something new to them both, and Hu didn't know how she would handle these two.

"No, thanks," Mei said. "I think we've gone the wrong way. Sorry to trouble you."

She bent down to turn the wheelbarrow around. But Rat's Teeth stood in the gateway, blocking the way to the street. He leaned on his spear, cleared his throat, and spat.

"Didn't know they bred 'em so nice in this pile of dog dung. What's yer hurry, missy? What've you got in there?" He looked at the sack in the wheelbarrow.

"Flour, sir," Mei answered.

"Ah, that'll be for the cook inside," Rat's Teeth said. "Boy!" he ordered Hu. "You take that in, while we have a chat with the girlie."

The big soldier guffawed. He reminded Hu of a large dog, panting and barking at nothing. Hu didn't like these soldiers. And he knew his family could not afford to lose the precious supplies they'd gotten on credit from the grain store. He picked up both handles of the wheelbarrow.

"It's our flour, not yours," he said. "And she's my sister, not your girlie." He made a sudden run for it, swerving around the soldier in the gateway.

But the big soldier swept his spear low in front of Hu's feet, nicking the flour sack with its blade. Hu tripped. He tried to hang on to the wheelbarrow handles to stop it from tipping over, but his trouser leg caught on the piked edge of the spear. A piece of cloth ripped away, and Hu fell. One elbow came down in a large, fresh pat of horse dung. And so did a pile of flour.

Mei grabbed the sack so no more could spill. She gave Hu a hand up. "Excuse us, please," Mei said in a dignified voice.

The two soldiers stood with their arms crossed over their spears, laughing loudly, still blocking the exit.

"Look!" Hu said suddenly, pointing to the top of the gateway. The men turned to see what Hu was talking about. Quick as a flash, Hu pushed the barrow wheel over the toes of the nearest soldier. Rat's Teeth hopped back and swore, while Hu and Mei bolted past him and out the gate.

They ignored the guards' yells and ran down the street as fast as they could without spilling the rest of the flour. Another group of soldiers was riding straight toward the hall. Hu and Mei ducked into a side alley to avoid them. They steered the barrow around piles of rubbish, bumped through potholes, and kept running. The flour sack bounced and tilted wildly. Several corners later they stopped for breath and looked back. There were no soldiers in sight, but they'd left a trail of white flour sprinkles.

"Think—we've—lost—them," panted Hu.

Mei checked the flour. "We've still got most of it. But you . . ." She looked at Hu.

One trouser leg was shredded from the knee down. Hu's bare and dirty knee poked through. Horse dung and flour were smeared all down his sleeve.

"Like my uniform, Commander?" Hu laughed, although he felt shaky inside.

"You think Ma's going to find that funny?" Mei said. "You can't perform for nobles looking like you've been manuring the fields. Those trousers can't be mended, and I bet you've grown out of your costume ones."

Hu's hopes fell in a heap. He hadn't thought of that. He wanted to perform with his family so badly.

"Listen. There is a way," said Mei thoughtfully. "Though you might not like it." She gave him a wicked look. "Let's see if you're game."

REN

Ren lay sprawled on the floor of the town hall's tower. He was listening to the singing that floated in on the summer air. The battalion's welcome banquet was going on in the courtyard below, and Ren was not invited. It was for adults only. He could hear the performance and he could smell the food, but the windows faced the wrong way and he couldn't see. Ren was lonely and annoyed.

The audience hooted and clapped. Ren wondered what story was being performed.

"O hark! O hear! In times of old
Lived an archer brave, a hero bold."

The Legend of Archer Yi! Ren knew that play. Once there had been ten suns, one for each hour. One day, when the Emperor of Heaven got angry, he sent all ten into the sky at once. Everything on earth began to burn up. So the Lady of the Moon told her famous husband, Archer Yi, and he brought out his bow to save the world. . . .

Ren got up and pushed the dusty window shutters farther open. In the kitchen yard he could see Lien chasing the cook's chickens, but he couldn't see the main courtyard next door. Above him there was a third story to the tower.

He'd probably be able to see the show from there, but the door was locked.

Dong-cha! went the gong. More clapping. There must be acrobatics to go with the singing, Ren realized. He straddled the windowsill and leaned outward. He could just see soldiers standing in a far corner of the main courtyard.

Ren was not going to miss out any longer. He put one foot cautiously onto the roof. The tiles held. He swung his other leg over the windowsill and climbed out. The roofing clinked. Ren held tightly to the sill.

Keep calm, he told himself. *Don't go too fast or you might slip.*

He could see the soldiers head to foot now. They were all watching the play. If they happened to look up, they would see him standing there too.

So Ren lay down cautiously on the knobbly pottery tiles. Under his body the roof was warm, baked in the sun. The warmth seeped into his muscles and relaxed him. He lay there for a bit, enjoying it.

Then the music started up again. Ren slithered forward on his stomach. He pulled himself up to the roof's corner ridge and looked over.

It was a great view. Ren could see much more than the play. He saw the roofs of the whole town—the tiled terraces of the hall, the magistrate's house, and the grain store, giving way to the higgledy-piggledy thatches of the market and the huts of the poor. Ren felt like an eagle in the blue sky. He saw everything, and no one saw him.

One story down, the Lady of the Moon began to sing again. Two girls launched into a series of backflips and handsprings. Archer Yi strode to the middle of the courtyard. He was played by a local man, dressed like a soldier and armed with a bow and arrows.

"Archer Yi fits an arrow to his bow. He draws and takes aim." The Lady tossed up a cloth ball. It burst into flames.

Archer Yi let fly. His arrow went straight through a hoop held by the girls and brought the burning ball down. The soldiers roared enthusiastically. Ren had to stop himself from cheering too.

"One unswerving arrow will bring down the ninth sun. One arrow will carry Archer Yi's fame to the heavens. The string thrums. . . ."

The last ball roared into flame and flew high into the air, way above the hoop. With a lurch in the pit of his stomach, Ren realized that Archer Yi was aiming straight in his direction. Ren ducked behind the corner ridge. The arrow whizzed into the tiles on his left and wedged there quivering. It was a very near miss.

While Ren lay dead still and trembling, Commander Zheng stepped forward and motioned for silence. Everything about Ren's father had the look of authority: from his gold-embroidered clothes to his badge of office. A long sword swung in a lacquer sheath from his belt, and one hand rested on the hilt. Beside him, the Beicheng Magistrate looked faded and shabby.

"Thank you, Magistrate Ding, for your excellent hospitality," the Commander began. "Thank you, people of Beicheng, for your warm welcome to the Imperial troops. As you know, we have come here to work. I look forward to your assistance." He nodded at the Magistrate, who bowed back.

"I would like to make a gesture of thanks," continued the Commander. "In the spirit of Archer Yi, I propose that the battalion hold an archery competition outside the town, at the Mid-Autumn Festival, in three months' time. I invite everyone to enter, including the people of your township. I will provide the prize myself. A horse each to the best archer and crossbowman."

"Ghosts alive!" said a voice directly below Ren. Ren started and almost slipped off the roof. He looked down into the kitchen yard. His eyes met those of one of the performing girls. Her makeup was streaked with sweat, and the bun in her hair tilted sideways. She looked at him in amazement.

"What are you doing here?" Ren asked, as the troops cheered.

"I could ask you the same question," she said.

"Who are *you* to ask *me* questions?"

"Who? Hu—you got it!" She laughed like a boy, not at all like Lien's giggles.

The girl was very rude, and she talked with a thick northern accent, as if she had a mouthful of food—Ren thought she was coarse. He worried she would give him away.

"I need our arrow," she said.

"You can have it—as long as you don't inform anyone that I'm here. And get out."

"Fine," she said. "You're a ghost, and I'm just seeing things. Chuck the arrow here."

Ren reached for the arrow, and tossed it to her.

But as he did, his other elbow knocked a tile loose. Ren felt it slipping. He reached for it, but it was too late. The tile slid slowly and surely toward the edge of the roof. It teetered there for a second, then flipped and fell into the main courtyard.

At just that moment, the Commander, the local Magistrate, and the deputies turned to walk under the eaves.

The tile smashed down on First Deputy's shoulder. He staggered.

The Commander and his officers whipped around and drew their swords. Then everyone in the courtyard looked straight up—at Ren.

HU

The Lis went home tired and happy, thinking more about the meal they'd been fed than the boy on the roof.

"A horse! A real horse!" Hu shouted as he entered their hut. "Ah-po, there's an archery competition, and the Commander's offering a horse!" Horses were rarer than gold. How rich was the Commander if he had two to spare?

"He said townspeople were allowed in the competition." Hu turned to his father. "You could win; I know you could!"

"Hmm, we'll see," said Li San.

"Aiya!" Ah-po fussed around, taking Mei's ribbons out of Hu's hair.

"If I get any proposals of marriage for my beautiful second daughter, what should I say?" Li San teased.

Everyone laughed, except Ah-po.

"Tell them she's not available, but your first daughter is," Hu said.

Mei flushed pink. He gave her back her trousers.

"It's not proper," grumbled Ah-po. "The spirits will get upset."

"Nah," smiled Li San. "It brought us a good feed. Nothing wrong with that."

"San-San—" Hu's mother finished counting the string of cash the Magistrate had paid them for the performance. She looked serious as she spoke to Li San. "What do you think they're here for? You heard what the Commander said—do you think there'll be a draft?"

"Probably." Li San looked less cheerful. Hu wondered what a draft was. "I don't think I'll be in that competition, Hu."

"And what about Hu? Could they call him up?" asked Ma.

A knot formed in Hu's overfull stomach. He stopped bouncing around.

There was a long silence from Li San. "They're not supposed to," he answered finally. "He's not old enough. And he's short for his age. But that doesn't always stop them. Maybe it's better if I take that," he nodded toward the cash, "and go speak to Nail Head."

Mei bit her lip. Ah-po tutted.

Ma took a deep breath and held out the money to Li San. "Heaven protect us," she said.

Hu didn't know what they were going on about. "What? What about me?" he demanded. His imagination took a flying leap and landed on a brilliant idea.

"I'll go in the archery tournament, if you won't. You could teach me," he said to his father. This competition was the chance of a lifetime. If he won the prize, the Lis would be rich and they'd never have to worry about anything again.

"Eh?" said Li San. "You, go in the tournament? How?"

Hu took a deep breath. "I could use Archer Yi's bow."

"Sorry, son, you won't win."

Hu had expected his parents to need some persuading, but not to be so discouraging.

Li San put an arm over his shoulders. "Tell you what—if you really want to try, I'll do what I can," he said. "I'll teach you the basics. How 'bout that?"

REN

After the soldiers had been dismissed from the banquet, Commander Zheng came upstairs. Ren waited for the inevitable. More than anything, he didn't want to face his father's anger. He wished he could escape, but the town-hall complex had no back door. Instead, Ren thought about how he could shift the blame.

The Commander stood in the doorway with his arms crossed. "Have you got anything to say?" he demanded.

"It wasn't my fault, sir," Ren pleaded. "A girl said — "

"What?" The Commander clutched his sword hilt. "No son of mine will offer pathetic excuses."

"I didn't do it on purpose," Ren mumbled. "I didn't mean to knock the tile down."

"You should never have been on the roof. You have injured my best officer. You have publicly disgraced our family. I will not suffer such behavior in this household again." Commander Zheng paused and glared at Ren. "It is time you were given a proper education. That might teach you how to behave."

A nobleman's education? thought Ren. Maybe something good would come out of this, after all. He summoned his courage. Perhaps, he thought, his next request might please his father, if Ren was only respectful enough in how he asked.

"Could I, sir . . . that is, could you—please—permit Second Deputy to teach me how to drive a chariot?"

The Commander shook his head dismissively. "Second Deputy has more pressing matters. I have someone else in mind. You are a danger to yourself and others. You will not leave this building until further notice."

Commander Zheng turned and walked out. Ren was left alone to wonder miserably if he would ever learn how to be an officer. How could he prove his worth when he was never given a chance?

He wasn't alone for long, though. Soon another figure darkened the doorway.

Master Wang, the secretary of the battalion's supplies, had arrived. In his long black robe, he reminded Ren of a spider.

"Master Ren—it is my pleasure," Master Wang began, "to announce that your honorable father, Commander Zheng, has appointed me as your tutor. For the mornings only, I will teach you the classics. In the afternoons, sadly, I have other responsibilities, so you can use the time to work through some math problems. As Confucius says, *To study and practice frequently, is it not a joy?*"

Ren's heart sank even further. Master Wang was as empty of joy as a soldier's pack was of books. Ren wished the tile had never slipped. He wished he could train with Second Deputy. He nearly wished he was back in the capital, but surely even Master Wang couldn't be as bad as the First Wife.

Master Wang sat down on the mat opposite Ren. From a cloth parcel, he unrolled brushes, an inkstone, another scroll, and a thin cane. He put the bamboo scroll on the floor in front of Ren and tapped it with a long fingernail. Then he picked up the cane.

"Confucius says, *A nobleman without integrity is like a chariot without an axle. . . .*" Master Wang quoted. He stopped abruptly. "Repeat!"

"Um, a nobleman what?" said Ren.

Master Wang's mouth pursed into a little sharp smile. His cane swished down across the fingers of Ren's left hand.

Sparks of resentment flew up inside Ren as he jerked his stinging hand away. Who did Master Wang think he was?

"You will call me 'sir.' *A nobleman without integrity is like a chariot without an axle,*" Master Wang quoted acidly.

He flexed the cane between his fingertips, paused, and leaned forward. His next words were deliberate and biting.

"Your father may be a nobleman, but you are *no one,* boy," Master Wang hissed. "You are merely the child of his Third Wife. Do you think Commander Zheng would have brought the children of the First Wife to this barbarous outpost? *You* must learn to respect the wisdom of your elders and betters."

The tutor's words hurt Ren more than the cane. Did his father really think so little of him? One day, Ren vowed, he would prove Master Wang wrong. He didn't need stupid books. What were bits of bamboo compared to weapons and horses? He wanted to shoot real enemies and lead real troops into battle. He would show them all that he could be a worthy son.

HU

For several days following the announcement of the competition, Li San kept his promise. He took Hu shooting, after morning chores and the midday rush at the noodle stall. They walked around the town walls to a field with a tree where Li San hung a bamboo hoop.

"First check your equipment," Li San always instructed. "See that the string's not frayed, the arrow feathers not bent . . . Right. Feet apart, square and solid. This isn't acrobatics. You're not about to go anywhere; only the arrow is. That's it."

Li San stood close behind, correcting Hu's hold. He helped Hu nock the arrow onto the string and draw the string to his cheek, over and over again.

"Don't pinch the arrow between your fingers, or it might come off the string. That's dangerous — it could fly anywhere. All right, let go . . . now!"

Hu's first shots went straight into the ground. Useless. Every day, Hu's hands got sweaty and his arms trembled from the effort. Eventually, one arrow skimmed the hoop. *Tomorrow,* thought Hu as they tramped home past the river boats unloading military supplies, *tomorrow I'll get one in.*

But the next morning a group of soldiers came down to the marketplace. The Li family watched them from the noodle stall. Hu recognized Big Ears and Rat's Teeth from the town-hall gate. They were led by an officer in polished armor and highly decorated boots, who stepped around the rotten vegetables and fish guts that littered the market square. The officer read from a list of names on a bamboo scroll.

"In the name of the Emperor, Magistrate Ding summons the following men: Potmaker Wang, Song Si, Liao and sons . . ." the list went on, "Li San, Fisherman Bing . . ."

Li San patted his wife's shoulder. "Not Hu, you see," he said.

Hu's mother nodded and hurried inside.

"Are you going now?" Mei asked him.

Li San nodded and smiled at her. "Look after Ah-po and your brother."

Then he folded his brown, muscled arms around Hu in a hug. "Keep practicing, try not to lose any arrows, and you'll make a good marksman."

"What do you mean?" said Hu. Something was going on that he hadn't been told about. As usual, Mei seemed to have figured it out, though. "Where are you going?"

"Old Hard-as-Nails has got someone to hammer him at last," Li San said in a low voice. "His Highness the Commander says the Great Wall needs repairing and he needs more people to do it. So the Magistrate's called up men from every family to work with the troops. It's called a draft. I don't know when I'll be back."

"Couldn't I go too?" Hu asked.

Li San shook his head. "Don't even think about it. It's no fun."

"How do you know?"

"I just know."

Li San knew a lot that he didn't let on, Hu thought. Some things about his father were a mystery. Hu knew, for example, that he didn't come from Beicheng, but he didn't know how he'd gotten there.

Ma came out with a bundle of stuff for Li San, wrapped in a sleeping mat.

"Here," she sniffed. She was about to cry, Hu thought.

"How long will you be gone?" Hu asked. He didn't like the thought of his father leaving them. His father, his family, was all he had.

Rat's Teeth sauntered up to the stall.

"Look who's here," he said nastily to Hu. "Our friend the flour thief."

Li San stepped between Hu and the soldier. "The boy's got nothing to do with this," he said. "He's not on the list." Then he turned to Hu, "I've been meaning to tell you, you can't go in the competition with that bow. It's no good. It's—"

But whatever else his father had been going to say was cut short. Rat's Teeth shoved Li San in the back with the butt of his spear.

"Move it!" growled the soldier.

Hu, Mei, and Ma watched the soldiers march the men out through the town gateway.

"Be grateful you're safe," said Ma. "Your father gave Magistrate Ding back the performance fee, so you don't have to go."

Hu felt guilty. He would gladly have gone up to work on the Wall to save his family the money. But they had spent it to save him. Now they had nothing left again. And his dad was gone. Hu hoped he would be all right.

To make things worse, something was wrong with the bow. He worried that the bowstring was getting frayed. Was that what Li San meant? Hu wondered. Was there anything he could do to help his family?

REN

Ren's father barely spoke to him all month. All day, every day, it seemed, the Commander and his officers (First Deputy with his arm in a sling) were up at the Wall. When they returned at nightfall, the Commander shut himself in his office downstairs. Ren spent his mornings writing and repeating texts about good behavior. The tutor also gave him *Nine Chapters on Mathematical Techniques* to work through in the afternoons, while Master Wang went to the stores and wrote up the battalion's accounts. Lien hung around and pestered her big brother to play.

Ren tried not to do anything wrong. But Master Wang still sneered and caned him for the tiniest mistakes.

One day, staring out the window after Master Wang had left, he noticed a boy outside town shooting arrows at a tree. Ren had had enough. Being good had gotten him nowhere — his father was too busy to notice him. Ren was not going to sit around and watch while some peasant kid practiced to win his father's prize. He longed to have a go himself.

Ren was not allowed out of the gate, and he knew the guards would see him if he tried to leave through it. But if he could just keep his nerve, he told himself, maybe the door was not the only way.

The next day, the boy was back. After lunch, when Lien and the cook were sleeping, Ren climbed out the window.

The roofs of the town were spread out beneath him. It was just like the day of the performance. His heart thumped. He was taking a big risk, but he was determined. Ren traced the intersections of the roofs: from the tower to the kitchen, kitchen to Magistrate Ding's, Magistrate's house to the grain store, grain store to the town's north gate. A path to freedom.

The tiles were hot. He dropped down from the tower to the kitchen roof, took a deep breath, and jumped across the gap to Magistrate Ding's.

Someone was talking under Magistrate Ding's eaves.

"What was that?"

Ren froze. He recognized that odiously polite voice.

"Only rats, Master Wang," said Magistrate Ding. "Rats in the roof. They're bad this year. Not a good time to be storing grain here, eh? Ha, ha!"

"Excellent," said Master Wang. "So you agree to my terms—an eighty-twenty split of the profit?"

"That's very steep, Master Wang."

"I will have transport expenses to meet, you understand. And you'd have nothing without me, I remind you, sir."

Ren couldn't hear Magistrate Ding's response.

"I can rely on you to show the utmost discretion, I'm sure. We need not trouble anyone else about this matter. Particularly anyone close to the Commander."

Ren bristled. What was Master Wang doing that needed to be kept secret from his father? He wanted to stay and find out, but Master Wang would be the worst possible person to discover him. Ren needed to get away quickly. He crawled across the Magistrate's house, flinching every time the tiles creaked, then leaped across to the grain store.

Slam! His knee crunched into the grain-store roof. He bit

his lip to stop himself from crying out. Painfully, he hauled himself up. The town wall rose in front of him.

The surface of the wall was crumbly and pockmarked. Trying to ignore his throbbing knee, Ren dug his fingers and toes into handholds carved by the weather. At the top he pulled himself over the battlements and sat down to get his breath. There were no soldiers guarding the north gate underneath him; it was bolted shut instead. Like every town in China, Beicheng had four gates, but Ren had heard Second Deputy complain that Magistrate Ding kept all but the south entrance closed so he wouldn't have to pay for guards.

Ren climbed down the outside of the wall, and he was out of Beicheng. He felt a flush of victory.

Limping slightly, he sauntered toward the peasant boy he'd seen from the tower window.

Close up, the boy was short and skinny. He stood straight as any archer, in bare feet and tattered trousers. He was concentrating on the target and didn't notice Ren. With one smooth action, he drew the bowstring back, his elbow high.

Ren didn't know what to say, so he cleared his throat. The boy jumped, and the arrow flew off, a long way wide of the target.

"Ghosts alive!" exclaimed the boy. "Where did you come from?"

Ren remembered hearing that expression not long ago. It must be something people out here said a lot.

"Over there," said Ren, waving his hand vaguely in the direction of Beicheng.

"Ah, yeah," the boy said. A knowing look came over his face. "I'm seeing things again. What are you doing here?"

"I want a turn," Ren answered. "Let me shoot."

"Oh, really? Who are you?" the boy asked.

Ren disapproved of the boy asking questions. People below you in the order of the world were not supposed to do that.

"You tell me your name and I'll tell you mine," Ren said haughtily.

"You already know mine."

Ren was insulted. "How could I possibly know a lowly peasant like you?"

The boy's eyebrows shot up. "Oooh!" he said, and laughed. Ren had an odd feeling he'd heard that laugh before. "I'm Hu, that's who," the boy said.

Ren had definitely heard that before. That was what the acrobat girl had said.

"Do you have a sister?" Ren asked the boy.

"Sure," the boy answered, laughing at him again. He seemed very cheerful under all that dirt. "But *she* didn't see you on the roof. *I* did."

Ren grimaced. He didn't want to talk about that. One of the worst days of his life was not any business of a peasant.

And Ren was still not sure who he was talking to. "Do girls learn archery out here?"

"Nah. I was in my sister's costume," said the boy. "I've grown out of mine so I borrowed it for the performance."

Ren thought he would never wear a girl's clothes. And if he ever had to, he would never joke about it.

"So what is your real name?" he asked the boy with the bow.

"I told you. It's Hu. Li Hu. As in 'Tiger,' 'cause that's the year I was born."

Ren was born in the year of the Tiger too. He was disappointed to find they were equal in age. He'd thought Hu was younger because he was small and thin.

"That doesn't look like a real bow to me," he said, pointing to Hu's weapon and trying to sound knowledgeable.

"'Course it is. Been painted, that's all."

"Well . . ." said Ren. He was about to propose something completely new. He'd never spoken to a peasant before, and he'd definitely never asked one for help. He doubted that it was a proper thing to do according to Confucius and all that, and he was certain Master Wang wouldn't approve. But Master Wang wouldn't know about it. Neither would the Commander, until Ren could surprise him with his newly learned abilities.

"The battalion is holding an archery competition," Ren continued, "and I want to enter it. I want to win. You can teach me." Ren felt he was making a big concession in admitting that he needed to be taught.

"What if I win?" Hu asked. He put down the bow and folded his arms.

It hadn't even occurred to Ren that a peasant like Hu might win — might possibly be better than the son of a nobleman.

"What would someone like you do with a horse?" he scoffed.

The acrobat boy frowned. He rocked on the balls of his feet, and his hands tensed.

"Why should someone like *me* share *anything* with you?" Hu asked. "Your fancy hairpin alone is worth enough to feed my family for months. And you won't even tell me your name, Master High-and-Mighty." His voice was quiet but hard as his fists.

"I'm Master Zheng Ren, son of Commander Zheng, of the Imperial Battalion." Ren hadn't meant to tell him that, but it had the right effect anyway. The boy stepped back and looked at Ren with respect, or envy.

"You're the Battalion Commander's son?"

Ren nodded.

"I won't hit you, then," Hu said. "Don't see why you need me to teach you archery, though," he went on. "I won't do it, neither. Good day to you, Master Ren."

He picked up his bow and arrows and ran off toward town.

Ren was shocked. It wasn't a good day; it was a miserable day. Why would a peasant refuse when Ren had made such an effort and taken such a risk to talk to him?

HU

Hu had decided to go and see his father on the Wall. He missed him, and he needed to find out what the problem was with the bow, in case that tall, nose-in-the-air kid was right and it somehow wasn't a proper weapon after all.

He carried the painted bow over one shoulder. On the other shoulder Ma loaded him up with baskets filled with fresh, uncooked noodles to sell and a bowl of homemade bean curd on a carrying pole. Hu groaned. Since the army had arrived, the price of flour had gone up and the Lis were back to one meal a day. It was hard to find energy to do anything extra.

"Give your father this," said Ma. "I'm sure he needs some good food."

Hu looked enviously at the bowl. Li San wasn't the only one short of good food.

"You go too," Ma instructed Mei. "Make sure he doesn't spill it. Or eat it."

"That's no place for a girl," Ah-po fretted, "with all those strange men."

"He'll look after me," said Mei, winking at Hu.

"Tell your father we're fine," Ma said.

It took Hu and Mei a good part of the morning to climb from Beicheng up to the Great Wall. The early air was sweet and cool, but the baskets were heavy.

They trudged through waist-high fields of ripening

grain, and eventually they reached the top of the ridge and the Wall. The last time they'd been there was the day the soldiers came. Back then, everything had been still and quiet, except for the cicadas singing and the tiger Hu thought he'd seen. If there had ever been a tiger, all the activity up there now would have warned it off. The Wall was swarming with people. The long grass was trampled, and the bushes had been slashed. Men stripped to the waist were pushing barrows of rubble and dirt.

A lot of repairs had been done to the watchtower. Large wooden bolts had been fixed on the door. Inside, Hu saw rows of crossbows and regular bows hanging up, and a set of different-colored flags. Quivers full of arrows were stacked on new shelves, and sleeping mats were piled in a corner. Jars of water and stacks of brushwood lined one wall.

"Can you tell me where to find Li San?" he asked a soldier.

"What are you doing here?" the soldier asked suspiciously.

"We're looking for Li San of Beicheng," Mei said sweetly.

"Here!" Li San called from the steps. "Come outside, both of you."

"Has something happened at home?" he asked Mei in a low voice as soon as they got out of the tower. He looked thinner and more anxious than he usually did, glancing sideways as he spoke. It made Hu uncomfortable too.

Hu and Mei shook their heads.

"No, it's all fine. Ma sent you this," Hu said, fishing the bowl of bean curd out of one basket.

"Eh," said Li San. "She's better than the Lady of the Moon, your mother. And you look more like her every day," he said to Mei. "You're as lovely as a vision from the gods."

Hu liked to hear his dad talk like that. It reassured him that things were all right.

"What do you do in there?" Mei asked, looking at the tower.

"I've been mending the pulleys. See that flag on the top? It has to be raised and lowered at set times each day. If the Wall is attacked, they can send signals to Beicheng and the other towers along the Wall by changing the color of the flag."

"Do you sleep in there as well?" Mei said.

"Nah, only the soldiers are garrisoned there, not the likes of me," said Li San. "The men from Beicheng sleep under there." He pointed to some low humpies built out of cut branches. "Not much better than a fox's hole, but all right while the weather's warm. How are you, Tiger?" he asked Hu. "Why'd you drag the bow up here?"

"You haven't told me what the matter with it is," Hu said. "Is it the string?"

"Eh? Well, that's no good either," said Li San, taking a quick look at it. "But I've mucked around with the bow as well, to make it safer for performing. See that man by the tower door, with a face as long as a donkey's? He's one of the battalion's bowyers. He might have a spare string, but we can't afford what he'd charge to get it properly fixed. Now, tell your mother everything's fine here too. I better go back to work." He hugged them both at once and turned and walked away around the tower.

Hu watched him go, then approached the unfriendly-looking soldier who squatted by the door, fiddling with a crossbow.

"Are you the bowyer?" Hu asked him.

The man spat in the dust. "What's it to you?"

"I've got a bow with a frayed string," Hu said.

"Better fix it," the bowyer said, without looking up.

"Could you?"

The bowyer shrugged. "I don't make no promises."

He took the bow from Hu and flexed it carefully. Then he turned it sideways, and scratched off some of the paint to see the wood underneath.

"What's this for?" he scoffed. "Shootin' butterflies? It's a toy, not a bow."

Some of the nearby soldiers laughed at him, but Hu was beyond embarrassment; he was desperate. He had to know if it could be fixed, if he could use the bow in the competition.

"What's wrong with it?" he asked.

"Someone's taken a layer off the arms. Easier to draw, but got no power. Yer arrows'll go about as far as a girl's throw."

The soldiers laughed again.

Hu felt weak at the knees. No way could a pretty, painted, half-strength bow win against professional soldiers. That meant all his practice so far was wasted, Hu thought despairingly. The black shadow of failure made him feel cold.

"Can you make it work properly?" Hu asked.

"Depends what ye pay me," answered the bowyer. "Take a lot of work."

Hu had no money. "How about a bowlful of noodles?"

The bowyer spat at the ground. "For three or four days work? Think I've got nothing else to do? Go home."

"A bowlful every day? Until you're finished."

"Leave it here," the bowyer said. "I'll see . . ."

It was hard for Hu to put the bow down at the soldier's feet. It meant a lot to him.

"A bowlful every day!" said Mei as they went home. "Where are you going to get them from?"

"Don't tell Ma," Hu said. "She'll only worry. If I eat a bit less for a few days, I can spare some. It's my only chance."

He didn't know how he was going to practice while the bowyer fixed his weapon. Another thought filled him with fear: what if the bowyer couldn't be trusted? What if he didn't do the job and Hu had no bow?

REN

Ren hadn't seen Hu from the window for several days. Not that it mattered, because Ren wasn't going back out there again anyway. He'd hated having to skulk back into town across the roofs, scraping his knees and baking in the sun, all for nothing. At least he hadn't been noticed.

Then one afternoon the cook came puffing up the stairs, one hand on his fat hips. Lien skipped along after him.

"Master Ren, come downstairs, if you please," said the cook.

"The guards at the gate want to talk to you," Lien added.

Oh, no, thought Ren. Maybe he'd been caught after all.

When he reached the courtyard, he found two guards holding Hu by the elbows.

"Excuse us, Master Ren," one of the soldiers said. "This boy seems to think he's got a message for you."

Hu might give me away, Ren thought angrily. What was he doing here? To make sure no one could hear what Hu said, he told the cook to take Lien away and ordered the soldiers back to their posts.

"What is it?" he asked, when they were alone.

"I've changed my mind," said Hu. "If you bring a bow from the battalion, I'll teach you how to use it. We'll share: equal turns of the bow, equal share of the prize."

A surge of excitement went through Ren. He was tempted to change his mind too, despite the difficulties and the risk.

"What can you do with half a horse? Eat it?" he said scornfully.

"Nah," Hu said coolly. "Sell it."

"I don't have a bow," Ren said.

"Me neither," said Hu. "I gave mine to your battalion's bowyer to fix, and I don't think he's ever going to give it back. Keeps saying it's not ready, so I have to pay him more noodles. I haven't got any money to buy another one."

"Neither do I," said Ren.

"Dog's fart," Hu retorted. "Your father has two horses to give away, and you think you can't get just one bow?"

"Shh!" said Ren. A nobleman's son *should* have a bow, he was sure. But he didn't. Nor could he ask for one, after the tile incident. He was too proud to admit this to Hu.

"I'll get one," Ren said. "But you have to help."

"At your service." Hu smiled and bowed.

"Come to the grain-store entrance tomorrow at cockcrow, while it's still dark," Ren told him.

"Why the grain store?"

"Because I say so. Make sure no one sees." Ren was not about to explain his plan to this dirty northern peasant. "That will be all." He waved Hu away and went inside.

Ren went upstairs and collected his writing tools. He came back down and walked softly to his father's study, past the living room, where Lien was asleep on a mat. The cook was snoring in the kitchen. The only other sounds were the occasional clucking of chickens or a whinny from the stables.

The study curtain was ajar. Ren slipped into the room and closed the curtain behind him.

He had not been into the study before. The Commander

was a well-organized man: his silk map hung on one wall, the ancestor tablets on another. On a low table in the middle stood a jar full of flat strips of wood, made for carrying messages. Writing brushes and an inkstone were laid out, ready to use.

But Ren didn't touch them. If he used his own writing tools, he wouldn't have to clean his father's afterward. He knelt on the carpet. He reached across the table and took one of the wooden message strips. Dipping his brush onto his inkstone, Ren wrote carefully:

Please issue one bow and one quiver of arrows to Company Number Eleven.

His hand was shaky, and some of the characters wobbled, but Ren was sure they were all correct. He looked around for his father's seal to authorize the order. It wasn't on the table.

Where is it? Where is it? Please don't let him have taken it with him, Ren breathed. He couldn't see it anywhere. The only place he thought it could be was in a bronze box over by the sleeping mat.

Ren listened. Still no sound but the chickens.

He tiptoed over and lifted the lid on the box. It was heavy. In the heat the metal had swollen slightly, and the lid stuck. He used more force and the lid slid off suddenly, landing with a clang on the floor and hitting his big toe. Ren bit his lip and screwed up his face, hopping silently on one foot.

He peered in. There was the seal, cushioned in silk. But it wasn't the only thing in the box. Next to the seal lay a tiger, cast in bronze. Half of a tiger, actually. It was the length of Ren's hand, but it looked as if it had been sliced from head to tail. The tiger's head was thrown back in a snarl, and its one eye looked straight at Ren.

He read the characters engraved on its back:

From His Imperial Majesty,
To Honorable Commander Zheng . . .

A shiver ran down Ren's spine. The tiger came from the Emperor.

The chickens outside began to cackle. Ren knew the chickens made that sound when they saw the two people who fed them—Lien or the cook. Someone was awake. Time was up. He shoved the tiger back in the box and grabbed the seal.

Hurriedly he dipped the seal into the red seal ink and stamped it onto the message he had written. He wiped the seal clean with his sleeve and put it back.

"Big Brother! Ren?" Lien was calling him. She was looking for him upstairs. He hid the wooden order inside his tunic fold and went out into the corridor.

"I'm down here," he called. "Getting a drink."

It was done. He would have his own bow and arrows to shoot with soon. And no one but the Emperor's tiger knew.

HU

The sky was just beginning to lighten the next morning when Hu wriggled out from between Ah-po and his sister. A slip of moon was still out, and the city gate was closed. As Hu walked through the market, the stalls threw long, spidery shadows in the starlight. A way off, outside the town walls, the river whispered. Hu was getting the creeps. Ghosts could get you if you were unlucky. The Wall was supposed to be the worst place for those. And the river, Ah-po said, because the people who'd drowned were looking for company. Hu shivered.

There were soldiers on duty outside the town hall. Hu went around the back streets to avoid them. He didn't want to get tangled up with Big Ears and Rat's Teeth again.

A dog barked as he walked past Magistrate Ding's gates. Strange how loud noises seemed in the dark. *There's no need to be jumpy,* he told himself. He wasn't doing anything wrong.

When he reached the grain store, the door was still barred for the night. Hu looked up and down the street, but Ren wasn't there.

Hu rubbed one foot against the other. Mornings were getting cooler. Autumn was on the way.

"Psst!" someone whispered. Hu looked around again. Ren was definitely not in the street. Hu's skin prickled.

"Here!" Hu looked up in the direction of the whisper.

There was a dark shadow in the curve of the roof's gable. "It's me."

Ren was on the roof again, lying on his stomach. Hu nearly laughed. Why on earth would he have climbed the grain-store roof? Noble people were peculiar, Hu thought. But his father always said the rich could do what they liked.

"Good morning," Hu said.

"Shh! Catch!" Ren answered.

He tossed a small flat stick toward Hu. He wasn't a very good shot—it hit the gable and bounced sideways. Hu jumped for it, but the stick skimmed over the tips of his fingers and clattered to the ground.

"Take it to the armory," Ren hissed.

Hu bent down and picked up the stick. He slipped it inside his tunic just as a guard came around the corner from the town hall, spear in hand.

"*Wei!* What's going on? Stand still or I'll throw!"

Hu stood still.

"What are you doing here?" demanded the guard.

Hu thought. He could tell the truth, but maybe he would have to hand over the stick. They might not get the bow, then, if this guard wanted to keep it for himself the way Rat's Teeth did with the flour. Hu decided to distract him. It didn't matter what the guard thought, really, so long as he didn't spear him or search him.

"I'm collecting mushrooms," Hu said.

"Mushrooms?" said the guard in disbelief. "At this time of night?"

"Yeah, for the doctor. For his potions. They, um . . . have greater powers if you collect them under a waning moon. It's the influence of the night spirits, you know."

The guard looked at him doubtfully.

He wasn't buying Hu's excuse, Hu thought. *When things go wrong, make the audience laugh,* his father always said.

"It's true," said Hu. "What do you call soup made by ghosts?"

The soldier didn't respond.

"Soup-ernatural," said Hu.

The soldier's mouth twitched. He leaned on his spear, listening.

"And what do you call bean curd made by ghosts? A supernatural bean! A supernatural being! Get it?"

"Don't make fun of the spirits," said the soldier. "It's not wise. 'Specially not before dawn."

Hu cast around in his memory for more jokes. "All right, then," he said. "Have you heard how one day the bow complained to the arrow? 'Why do I have to do all the hard work?' said the bow. 'Because you're so highly strung,' said the arrow."

The man smiled.

"What do you call an ambitious arrow?" Hu asked.

The soldier shook his head. "Don't know."

"A highflier."

The soldier laughed. "I'll tell that one to our Second Deputy," he said. "Now, get out of here, boy, while I'm being generous. I'll flay your backside if you try collecting anything around here again."

This time the soldier returned to his post. Hu left for home, with the stick still tucked inside his tunic. From the corner of his eye, he saw a shadow flit across the grain-store roof toward the hall.

REN

"The roof ghost strikes again," said Hu when Ren joined him outside Beicheng in the afternoon. "Here you go." He offered Ren the bow and a quiverful of arrows. "I did what you said. The officer in the armory looked me up and down. He said he was surprised Company Number Eleven needed it."

"What did you say to him?" Ren was anxious.

"I told him a joke so he wouldn't think about it."

"You're good at that," Ren said grudgingly.

Ren took the weapon and fitted the arrow the way Hu showed him. It was the first time in his life he'd ever held a loaded bow. He drew back the string and felt the bow's strength resisting him. When he couldn't hold it any longer, he let go. The arrow skidded into the ground with a speed that startled him.

"Good, isn't it?" said Hu. Ren knew he wasn't talking about the shot itself, which was way off. He meant the soft, deadly whoosh of the arrow, the exhilaration of the bow's pent-up power.

Ren tried again.

Hu gave him tips on what to do.

"Don't grip the bow so hard," Hu said. "Loosen your fingers and lean your arm into it, or else you'll move the arrow off target, my dad says."

Ren frowned. Shooting wasn't as easy as it looked, and he didn't like to do poorly in front of Hu.

"It's hot," he complained.

"Hurry up—my turn again," said Hu.

Ren collected the arrows. As he walked back toward Hu, he glanced up at the Great Wall, twisting across the mountains. He wondered how long the repairs to the Wall were going to take. A while, he hoped, so everyone would stay out of town and he could practice with nobody around. He needed a lot more practice yet, he thought, before he could make his father proud of him.

Then he saw a group of men on horses riding down the path from the Great Wall—battalion officers. Ren broke into a run.

"Quick! We've got to hide," he yelled to Hu.

"Hide?"

"Yes! They'll see us!"

All around was open ground. There was nothing taller than knee-high grass to hide behind. If the officers told the Commander they'd seen him out here, he'd be dead.

"I know another way back into town," said Hu. "A cunning rabbit has three burrows, you know. Round the corner."

The boys sprinted for the town wall, then ran for a shed leaning against it—the one bit of cover between themselves and the front gate. The shed had a rickety ladder on top, for climbing up the town wall.

"We haven't got time to climb up there, not carrying the bow as well," Ren panted.

"We can hide inside, if you really want," Hu answered.

When they got closer, Ren recognized the shed by the stench. It was a public toilet. A cloud of fat flies hung around the doorway. Ren gagged.

"Welcome to the poor people's palace," Hu said, ducking inside.

"Revolting," Ren groaned. "I'm not going in any further."

"As you please, Master Prim-and-Proper," said Hu, looking out. "They're coming this way."

Ren held his nose and swatted away the flies.

"Step carefully," said Hu, laughing.

"Stop it! This is serious," said Ren.

"I am serious," said Hu. "One wrong step, and a terrible fate awaits you."

Hu didn't realize how right he was, Ren thought.

The boys could hear hooves approaching. They shuffled farther inside and pressed themselves up against the toilet wall. The hot, stinking darkness buzzed with flies. Ren tried not to breathe.

Outside, hooves trotted right up to the shed and stopped. Ren stiffened.

"All yours, comrade," said Second Deputy's voice. "We'll go ahead."

Someone dismounted with a thump.

"Here, give me a hand with my sword, will you?" That was First Deputy, the man Ren had injured. He, of all the officers, would be least sympathetic. Ren heard the metallic clink of a buckle being undone. Leather creaked, and First Deputy's footsteps approached the shed. "Puke!" he said, stopping short of the doorway. "Stinks enough to kill your grandmother."

Ren shut his eyes, as if that could stop First Deputy from seeing him. This was it—he'd probably be on the next boat home to the capital.

Next second, he felt Hu's hand clamp over his mouth. Then Hu began to scream.

"Aaagh!" he shrieked, bursting out through the door and

startling First Deputy, who'd been just about to step inside. "Aaagh! A snake! There's a snake in there," he yelled at the officers outside.

Ren peered through the dimness. He couldn't see any snake. The officers laughed. Ren could hardly breathe.

"Bite your bottom, did it?" said First Deputy. "Hey, Second Deputy, pass me back that sword. I'd rather wait until we get back to the hall." The men laughed again.

"*Ya!*" The riders urged their horses on and trotted off.

Hu gave a whistle like a wild goose. "Road's clear."

Ren sighed in relief and stepped out into the sunlight. "That was close," he muttered, wiping his feet on the grass. "I am never going in there again."

"Lucky you, to have a choice!" Hu said.

HU

Hu and Ren practiced shooting together most afternoons. Hu looked forward to it, even though Ren was a prickly companion, always jittery about something. Hu didn't completely trust him.

Ren always brought the bow, but twenty days out from the tournament, Hu saw a chance to get his own bow back. "Let's go up to the Wall today instead," he said. "My sister's got a customer she knows who can hurry the bowyer up."

Ren looked reluctant.

"It's all right for you. What if in the competition they won't let us share the bow?" said Hu. "Then you'll have one and I won't. Tell you what, we could go shooting near the Wall—on the far side, where nobody goes. Then I can see the bowyer afterward."

The boys climbed up between the millet fields. The grain was high, nearly reaching their shoulders.

"My dad says this should be harvested," said Hu, halfway up, "but there aren't enough people to do it."

"They're lazy," Ren said.

"Nah. They're working on the Wall."

The boys came up to the top of the ridge. Just a stone's throw away, dozens of men were lined up, pounding earth with thick poles. Most of the breach in the Wall had been leveled.

"There's my father!" Hu said. He started to wave.

Ren yanked on Hu's clothes to pull him down and dropped to his stomach among the grain stalks. "Keep out of sight, you idiot!"

"What for?" For someone who liked to act superior, Ren was always skulking around, Hu thought. "If you're really the noble son of Commander Zheng, why all this hiding?"

"Of course I am." Ren flushed. "It's just . . . he doesn't know I'm entering the competition. But if I can win, my father will approve. I think. He should."

Hu suddenly felt sorry for Ren. Li San wasn't like that — he encouraged most things Hu did. He was kind and funny, and Hu missed him. He only got to see his father for a few minutes at a time now.

"My tutor is already suspicious," Ren continued. "He knows I'm sneaking out. He just doesn't know when or how yet. The other day he said, 'You're turning black as a peasant, Master Ren. You should beware this northern sun.'"

Hu laughed. "Well, if I were Archer Yi, I could fix that." He squinted at the sun and pretended to shoot it. "We're nowhere near that good yet, though. Come on, there's less people over that way."

"I think I'm getting pretty good," said Ren.

"Yeah, you always think you're pretty good," Hu said. "More practice never hurt anyone —"

"'My father always says.'" Ren finished in a mocking voice.

"My father knows a lot," Hu said. "You're not better than other people just because you happen to be born noble. Anyone can wear a fancy hat and give orders. They don't have to carry them out. We do all the real work. Without us, you nobles are nothing."

"Who says? Your father?" said Ren nastily. "Not obeying orders is a crime."

"How come we have to have the army here anyway?" Hu said. "All the town's men are working on the Wall. And there's even less to eat than before. My dad says someone is cheating them out of their rations."

"Really?" said Ren.

"And if someone's stealing, there'll be big trouble. Whoever it is might get flogged or sent off into the desert. Sometimes their whole family gets punished."

Ren nodded. "Dishonor and disgrace," he said. "I hear plenty about that."

The boys reached the breach in the Great Wall at the end farthest from the watchtower. They clambered up the large mound of crumbled clay covered in weeds.

"What's on the other side?" Ren asked.

"Hills . . . forest." Hu waved one hand vaguely. "Don't worry. We won't get lost. I know this place like Archer Yi's wife knows the moon."

REN

On the far side of the Wall, the hills were hazy blue in the summer sun, and the forest was quiet, except for birds and insects. It occurred to Ren that if they could climb up the Wall so easily, it wouldn't keep much out. He was uneasy.

"Aren't there barbarians out there?" he asked.

"Must be some somewhere," said Hu. "On the plains past the hills, I s'pose. I've been here lots of times, and me and my sister have never seen anyone. Not even a ghost. Ah-po believes the bodies of the convicts who died building the Wall are buried under it. She says they come out looking for vengeance."

Ren looked at the rubble beneath his feet. It was creepy to think he could be treading on someone's grave.

Ren knew the Great Wall marked the edge of civilization. He had never been outside Han lands. Not even his father's soldiers came out here without special permission. He had the feeling that if he crossed this boundary, the consequences could be severe. If it was found out that he'd left the town hall, he could be beaten, but there were worse possibilities. Ren could be sent back to the capital. Or he could be thrown out on the street—disowned forever.

But a life imprisoned in the study with Master Wang would be miserable too. The whole reason for learning to shoot had been to impress his father and get him to include

Ren in the battalion's activities. Ren was sure he was on his way to achieving that—his archery skills were definitely improving. Besides, Hu was right; there wouldn't be anyone to see them on the Wall's far side. He pushed his lurking unease to the back of his mind and set off after Hu toward a clearing in the forest. They picked out a thick pine tree without low branches and used it as their target.

"The muscles between my shoulder blades are tight as bowstrings," Ren complained after a while.

Hu thumped him on the back. "This is what you call trial and errow," he said.

"Ha, ha," said Ren. Hu was grubby and coarse, but he had a way of making you smile sometimes.

They lay down on the grass for a rest.

"Something's not quite right," said Hu. "The birds are twittering too much." He sat up and looked at the forest around them. There was not a breath of wind.

"Curses! I forgot to do my homework," Ren moaned, suddenly remembering. "My tutor, Master Wang, set it. I brought it with me because I've got to get it finished."

He pulled a bamboo scroll out from the fold of his top and unrolled it.

Hu peered over Ren's shoulder. "What's that say?"

"It's the first part of *Nine Chapters on Mathematical Techniques*. I've only done about half. These problems are designed to kill, I tell you. Listen: *From the capital Luoyang to Wuzhong is three thousand miles. A fast horse sets out on the journey. On the first day the horse travels one hundred and fifty miles, afterward increasing its speed by fifteen miles each day . . .*"

"I know where Wuzhong is," Hu said. "That's the big town three days downriver from here."

"Brilliant," Ren said. "Any idiot knows that."

"Pity that tutor of yours doesn't teach you to be nice to people," Hu said.

Ren scowled. "Who cares about being nice to people? What I have to work out is: *How long will it take the messenger to return to the capital again, with a slow horse on the way back?*"

"How long did it take you to get here?" Hu asked.

"Under a month, with carriages and carts. That's much slower than horseback."

"Well, that would make the return trip a bit over a month, wouldn't it?"

"You can't do math like that," Ren said impatiently. "You have to be exact. The answer will be something like: *On the third watch of the twenty-ninth day.*" He began scratching characters in the dirt with a stick.

Hu lay on his back again. "Look at the color of the sky," he said. "See in the west? It's turning yellowish, like the inside of a pottery bowl."

"Shh," said Ren. He scribbled and calculated, while Hu hummed a tune. Thunder rumbled in the distance.

"We better go see the bowyer," Hu said.

"Wait. I'm halfway through."

By the time Ren got the answer to the horse problem, a breeze was stirring the tops of the trees. "Come on," said Hu.

Ren refused. "I've got to do the next one."

"Summer's about to end," warned Hu. "The dry's going to break."

"Twelve scoops of grain per horse per day and two per man . . ." muttered Ren.

A loud clap of thunder interrupted his thoughts. The boys looked up. The sky was bruised purple, with shots of gold sunlight breaking through the clouds.

"I told you," said Hu. "Summer's about to end *right now*. Better run for it."

The first drops of rain began to fall as the boys scrambled back over the Wall. The rain steamed as it splashed on the warm clay.

The millet field smelled of hot, wet earth. The ripe heads of grain tossed in the wind. The drops fell harder and faster. Lightning flashed around them. Ren clutched his homework to his chest under his tunic, leaned forward to protect it, and broke into a run.

"It's hailing," Ren yelled. The little stones pinged off them.

"Now we know what it feels like to be under fire!" Hu shouted back as they pelted down the hill toward the town.

秋

AUTUMN

REN

Ren was soaked. Sheets of water poured from the eaves of the tower above and drenched him as he returned to the study. Water ran off him into dirty puddles on the floor. He slopped his mud-soaked shoes off.

If he walked around like this, he would leave an obvious trail of yellow mud, he thought. There was nothing for it but to strip, then get clothes from the room next door. Quickly. What he didn't need was his little sister walking in or, even worse, Master Wang.

Ren took *Nine Chapters on Mathematical Techniques* out of his tunic and tossed it on the floor. He took off his top and wrung it. Black water ran out.

Ren looked at his right hand. His palm was dyed black. A cold trickle of horror ran down his spine. He picked up the instructional scroll, and more black water ran down his wrist. Ren picked open the wet strings with shaking hands and unrolled Chapter One.

It was gone. One whole chapter of math problems and half a chapter of his answers had been washed into a big black smudge.

Ren half gasped and half sobbed. He was going to be belted for sure. Tears of tiredness and unhappiness ran down his cheeks. *Pull yourself together,* he told himself. He pulled off his trousers and scrubbed his hands and face fiercely with the dripping trouser legs.

He was about to wring out his wet hair when he saw a figure standing in the doorway. Master Wang! He quickly held his wet clothes in front of his naked body. Master Wang looked at Ren with eyes that burned with contempt.

"I—I—I'm about to get changed," Ren stammered.

"So I see," said Master Wang. "Perhaps you would like to explain your state as soon as you are dressed. And show me your completed homework."

"I can't," whispered Ren. He looked at the sodden scroll on the floor. "The book got wet. The characters . . . are . . . washed away."

"They are *what*?"

"Washed away!" Ren shouted. "It's not my fault. I didn't mean to damage it." If Master Wang wasn't so mean, this would never have happened, Ren reasoned.

Master Wang flicked his fingernails. Ren had the nasty impression that he was sizing Ren up like a sum on an abacus—as if he knew Ren's number exactly, and what to do with him.

"A single book, Master Ren," said the tutor in his softest and most venomous voice, "is worth more than you will ever be. Meet me downstairs. At the door to your father's study."

Master Wang left. Ren dragged his tired body to the chest of clean clothes in the room next door. Lien was there, sitting cross-legged in front of an arrangement of dolls.

"Don't say anything," Ren said.

She sat in silence, wide-eyed, until he had dressed.

"Are you in trouble, Big Brother?" she asked, patting him on the arm.

Ren felt he was going to choke. He nodded.

"With our father?"

"I'm going to be. Listen, Lien—he might send us away. Don't tell on me, will you?"

Lien looked frightened. She shook her head and put her hand on his.

Ren shrugged off her hand and went downstairs. He could hear his father talking with the deputies in the study. Ren walked slowly, putting off the inevitable meeting as long as possible.

". . . rot will ruin the crops," came the Commander's voice. "We may have to cut rations. Who knows how long those scribblers in the Grain Ministry will take to organize more supplies . . ."

Master Wang was listening at the curtained entrance.

Eavesdropper, thought Ren. Suddenly he remembered the time when he had eavesdropped on Master Wang—that had been about grain too. Ren wished he had stayed to hear more details. He was certain of one thing: Master Wang had not wanted the Commander to know.

Ren crept up on the tutor. Heart in his mouth, he made a blind gamble.

"Are you worried he might have found out your secret?" he whispered.

The tutor jumped. His eyes narrowed. "I beg your pardon, Master Ren?"

Ren repeated himself.

"I don't know what you're talking about," Master Wang protested. But he spoke very quietly, so the men on the other side of the curtain wouldn't hear.

"Yes, you do," said Ren, just as softly. He had a feeling he was on to something, although he didn't really know what. "The grain and Magistrate Ding?"

Master Wang moved away from the Commander's door. His thin fingers gripped Ren's arm like a claw.

"You and I will reach an understanding," he hissed. "Your silence for mine. I will turn a blind eye to your misadventures, even though I have finally caught you out. You will keep your mouth shut on all matters concerning myself."

Ren nodded. "Done."

A shiver of relief went through him. He had bluffed and won. Master Wang would not tell on him, and Ren would not be disgraced. He was safe. Ren felt like a bowstring that had just been released and was quivering in the middle. He also felt a wicked delight at having power over his tutor.

Abruptly, the Commander pulled the curtain aside.

"Ah, Master Wang," he said. "I need you to calculate how long our current supplies will last and suggest what we can do to stretch them out. As a matter of urgency."

"Certainly, sir." Master Wang bowed.

Commander Zheng looked at Ren.

"Oh, Ren. Instruct the cook to make a hot meal for four. I have business to discuss."

Ren nodded respectfully. "Yes, sir."

As he passed his tutor in the corridor, Master Wang hissed at him. "You'll keep, boy. There are other accounts to settle for now."

HU

The rain bucketed down all night and for the next two days.

"The spirits are tipping out their basins," grumbled Ah-po. "Too much rain's a bad omen. Somebody's offended the Emperor of Heaven."

The third afternoon it stopped. But the sky was gray, and everything dripped.

Mei came back empty-handed from a trip to the grain merchant. "The price of flour has doubled," she announced. "The hail's damaged the crops, and there's an order from the Magistrate—*Imperial prerogative*."

"What does that mean?" asked Hu.

"It means the army gets the food," Mei answered.

"It means things are bad," Ma said.

"*Ai!*" said Ah-po. "I told you so."

"You'll have to go up and see your father," Ma went on. "While the weather's eased up. See if he has grain rations he can spare. Take him some bean curd to eat instead."

"Our little Mei shouldn't be going up there," Ah-po said. "Nobody will want to marry a girl who hangs about with soldiers."

"I'll go with her," said Hu. He still needed to get his bow back from the bowyer.

"Stay away from the soldiers," warned Ma.

As if that was likely, Hu thought. Soldiers on the Wall were as avoidable as ants in an ant nest.

No one else was out when Hu and Mei plodded into the sludgy fields. The wind was cool.

"It's autumn, all right," said Mei. "When's the archery competition?"

"Mid-Autumn Festival—next full moon," said Hu.

"That makes it less than twenty days away. Watch out behind you!"

A soldier on horseback, carrying a flag on a pole, was approaching at a quick trot. Several other mounted men came after him. Hu and Mei cleared off the path.

The riders clattered past, splattering mud over the Lis.

"That was Commander Zheng behind the standard-bearer," said Hu. "He's got the only white horse in the battalion."

"How do you know?" said Mei.

"His son told me," Hu answered.

Mei's eyes widened. "You've been talking to the Commander's son? Is that a good idea? We're not supposed to go near the soldiers even, let alone the Commander's family."

"He's only a kid," Hu said, "like us. We practice archery together. Without him, I wouldn't have a bow. I want to win this competition, Mei. You don't want to be stuck in the smelly old market making other people's noodles forever and ever, do you? I don't."

Mei sighed. "Me neither. We've got to make the most of every opportunity, I suppose. But be careful mixing with him, little brother."

When they got near the Wall, Mei stopped and retied her hair. "Is there any mud on my face?" she asked, wiping her forehead with a corner of her sleeve.

"What does it matter?" Hu asked.

Mei didn't reply.

Leaning against the watchtower door was Big Ears, one of the soldiers from the town hall, shoveling food into his mouth with chopsticks.

"Oh, no. Not him again," said Hu.

"He's not so bad," Mei said. "He's nice to me."

Hu looked at her. "Now who needs to be careful of the company they keep? You don't *like* him, do you?"

"He's a customer," she said defensively. "Don't be rude about him. Besides, how else do you think we'll get the bow back?"

The closer they got to the soldier, the less she looked at him and the more shy she seemed. He was watching a group of soldiers squatting in a circle outside the tower. They seemed to be playing a game using a pile of short sticks with characters scratched on them, scattered on the ground.

"Excuse me," Hu said as they approached the men.

"Afternoon, missy," said Big Ears, ignoring Hu. "Here on business?"

Mei nodded. As she did, the ribbon in her hair fell out, and her carefully tidied hair fell loose.

The soldier bent down awkwardly, slopping his food and dropping his chopsticks in the dirt. He picked up Mei's ribbon and offered it to her as if she were the Empress.

Mei went bright pink as she took it. "We've come to collect our property from the bowyer," she said.

"Oh, right, right," said Big Ears. "I've found where he keeps it. Be right back."

He was going to go into the tower, but one of the soldiers in the circle grabbed his trouser leg.

"Where do ye think yer off to? It's your turn." The soldier gathered up the sticks on the ground and put them in a cup. Big Ears shook it, closed his eyes, and tipped the sticks on the ground.

"Eh! Ya got 'fire' on top, ya great turtle." The soldiers were laughing at Big Ears. "Things are looking good—a 'woman' as well, hey!"

"*Aiya!*" The big soldier shuffled his feet in embarrassment. Trying not to look in Mei's direction, he went off to find Hu's bow.

"Want a throw, boy?" asked the soldier in charge of the game. He offered Hu the cup. "Smallest bet's two coins; 'fire' and 'tiger' win."

"I haven't got any money," Hu said.

"That food'll do," said the soldier. "Put in yer potful of bean curd; we'll put in two copper cash each."

Hu was afraid they might not be so friendly if he said no. Besides, it was worth a go. He might win the money. If Hu won cash, he could buy something to eat in the market, something like onion bread or soy eggs or even duck wings. . . . He was so hungry. He took the cup and shook it, then tossed the sticks into the middle of the circle. Mei gave him a kick in the shins, but Hu ignored her.

The soldiers looked at the characters. Hu couldn't read them, but they weren't the same as Big Ears's. The soldiers weren't smiling anymore. The man who'd passed Hu the cup gave him a strange look—hostile, even fearful.

"Ya've got a 'tiger,'" he said, "but it's under the 'north snake.' And 'darkness.' That's a bad lot of sticks ya've thrown, boy. They're a sign. Now clear out before ya bring bad luck on all of us. And don't come back."

Hu took the bow Big Ears held out and hurried after Mei.

"Now you've gone and lost our dad's dinner," his sister hissed at him. "And we won't be able to talk to him anymore."

It was bad luck, not winning the money, and even worse luck not to be allowed to see Li San. Hu was silent. He didn't know exactly what the 'north snake' or 'darkness' was, but sometimes it felt like fate was stacked against him. Like there really was something out there, lying in wait to drag him down.

REN

The day of the Mid-Autumn Festival dawned fine and cool. Commander Zheng came upstairs to Ren's study to check the weather. Trails of mist curled around the hills and the Wall, silvery in the early sun.

"Like the mountain of the Immortals, isn't it?" the Commander said to Ren with a smile. "Perfect conditions for the archery meet. I see First Deputy's got the targets set up in the field already. Are you coming down to watch?"

His father was allowing him out! Ren could have hugged him with happiness, but he didn't dare.

"Yes, sir! I'll come later. After the registration."

The Commander nodded. "We'll see what the Tiger Battalion marksmen can do, eh?"

"Yes, sir." Ren smiled. An uncertain smile. His stomach was quivery again. More than anything, he wanted his father to see what he could do. He felt almost sick with excitement. For a moment he wanted to share with his father how hard he'd trained and how much he'd achieved in spite of all the difficulties. "You do me proud, son," he might say. Ren wished he would.

But it was far more likely that his father would ground him again for disobedience. Especially if he knew how Ren had escaped over the rooftops. And how he'd used the seal to get the bow. And followed Hu out over the Wall. No, he could never let the Commander know all that. Ren would be completely disgraced. The only thing his father needed to know, could ever know, was that Ren had won the competition.

Ren was silent. The Commander went downstairs, and shortly afterward Ren saw him riding out with the deputies and Master Wang.

Master Wang hadn't said anything further about the day he'd caught Ren soaking wet. Lately, the tutor had been busy organizing supplies of everything from grain to building timber. He was too preoccupied to give Ren instructions about what he could or couldn't do at the festival. So Ren thought he could do what he liked, once the way was clear.

At last the cook set off with Lien, fussing after the food baskets. Ren set off too—through the town-hall door for the first time in months. He was full of hopes as shimmering and untouchable as the morning mist.

This time, the boys had arranged for Ren to meet Hu at the Lis' house. He gave their prearranged signal—the wild-goose whistle—and Hu appeared. Not only did Hu have his own bow, he also had an old set of leather armor, a battered hat, and a false mustache draped over one arm.

Ren stared at Hu's props. This time Hu was being ridiculous, he thought.

"Come inside," said Hu. "My family's gone to find my dad, 'cause all the men on the Wall have the day off to watch. Ah-po's a bit slow, so they went early."

"You're not going dressed in those, are you?" Ren asked, pointing at Hu's gear.

"No, I'm not. You are." Hu answered.

"What? I'm not going like that." He looked at Hu in amazement. What sort of a fool would he look in that old gear? Hu might not have any sense of dignity, but he did.

"Oh, so you're not going, then?" Hu raised his eyebrows in mock surprise.

"Of course I am," Ren responded.

"So how exactly are you going to go and not get found out?" said Hu. "If you just go as you?"

Ren hadn't even thought about that. He was allowed out, but he didn't have permission to shoot in the competition.

He swore. "I can't miss out," he said passionately. "I won't. I've never wanted anything more than to win this tournament." Today of all days he was not going to be bundled back to the town hall like a naughty little boy.

"So," Hu continued, "you're sure you want to go? 'Cause you'll either have to get your father's permission or wear this." Hu held out the costume to Ren.

Ren took a deep breath. "I'll do whatever it takes," he said. He took the gear reluctantly. "Such old-fashioned armor," he grumbled.

"It's secondhand," said Hu, while he pasted the mustache on Ren. "My father picked it up somewhere years ago. We use it for Archer Yi and all the military roles."

Hu looked at his handiwork. "Your skin's a bit too nice," he said. He took a handful of soot from inside the *kang* and rubbed it into Ren's face and neck.

"Now you'll blend into the crowd. Except those'll be a dead giveaway."

Hu pointed to Ren's trousers, visible from the thigh down. They were silk—the deep black of midnight, with a rich sheen.

"Lend me a pair of yours," Ren said.

Hu shook his head. "Can't. I've only got one. My mother's saving up to make me a new pair for winter." Then he grinned. "My sister's got a spare pair—you know the ones

I wore the first time you saw me? But she'll be mad if anything happens to them. You can only have them if you return them." Hu lifted the lid off a basket in the corner and fished around inside.

"Here. They're her costume pants," he said, pointing to the flowers embroidered down the leg.

"I'm not wearing those!"

Hu was still grinning. "Turn them inside out and tuck the bottoms into your boots. You'll be fine. Very fine indeed, madam — I beg your pardon — sir!" Hu put his hands together and bowed deeply, just like Magistrate Ding or Master Wang.

Ren laughed, then he sneezed. The false mustache tickled his nose.

"Stop making me laugh, or I might lose this thing." Ren twirled the ends of the mustache.

That sent Hu into fits. "Ha! Ha!" he said, nearly choking, "It's Commander Zheng junior! Tenth Deputy — no — Renth Deputy!"

"All right, come on," said Ren impatiently. He felt like an idiot, all dressed up in inside-out girls' clothes and an old costume, with a low-class pauper laughing at him. What nobleman would put up with that? But Hu was right — if he wanted to compete, he would just have to suffer it.

"Let's get down there and enlist," Ren said, "before we miss out."

HU

The drums were rolling to marshal the competitors as Hu and Ren approached the competition site. The remains of the millet had been cleared from the terraced field on Beicheng's north. A series of straw bales were lined up as targets. A hundred paces back from the targets, a scorched line in the earth showed the competitors where to stand.

The battalion's banners flew on either side of a pavilion facing the field.

"That's where my father and the Magistrate will be," Ren said. He was fiddling nervously with his mustache.

"Leave it alone," said Hu. "Costumes are like chicken pox: it's better if you don't scratch. Where do we go to join in, do you think?" Hu was excited, and a bit nervous too.

Ren pointed to another banner, on the near side of the pavilion. A sea of men surrounded it, shoving and calling out.

"I can't see any officer taking names," Hu said.

"I can't either," Ren said. "But he's in there somewhere. So we've got to find him."

"Like a needle in the ocean," Hu commented. "Near impossible to find." It was also near impossible to win against a whole battalion of soldiers, Hu thought. He had felt so confident shooting with Ren, sending his arrows whizzing through the hoop. Now he was going to be put to the test.

The two boys stood on the fringe of the field and watched

the throng before them. Hu thought how bright and tiny was their hope of winning. If they could only pull this off, he and his family would be rich forever.

"Well —" Hu said. "All great heroes defeat impossible odds." He hummed the Archer Yi song: *"O hark! O hear! In times of old, lived a hunter brave, a hero bold."*

"But it's not 'times of old' anymore," said Ren.

"We can still be bold, though," said Hu.

Ren nodded. "Here goes."

The crowd of men seethed like the river in flood. Most were trying to push their way inward. The few who'd gotten their names down were trying to push their way out. Everyone was shouting to be registered: "Zhou from West Lakes!" "Young Mao the vegetable seller!"

"Mind your mustache," Hu said in Ren's ear. He began to squirm his way through. Because he was small, he could weave between the adults. Then Hu got squashed between two soldiers. The metal studs in their armor pressed into his face. Arrows sticking out of a quiver poked him in the neck. He couldn't breathe. The crowd surged, carrying him sideways. One of the soldiers elbowed Hu, pushing him back, and he was out on the fringe of the crowd again, shaken and bruised.

Hu rubbed his scratched face. He couldn't see Ren. He called but didn't hear an answer. He would have to wait, or he might get killed in the crush. But what if they closed the list because there were too many people?

Eventually the crowd thinned, and there was Ren, at the front at last. Hu came up beside him.

"Next!" called the officer. "Where are you from? Are you old enough?" he snapped. Hu hadn't known there was an age limit. He thought the only thing that mattered was whether he could shoot.

"I'm from Beicheng," he answered.

"What's your surname?"

"Li."

"Are you on the town's list of men?"

"Should be," Hu said. He was a few years too young, of course, but he was good enough to beat most of the locals, he was sure.

"Full name?" said the officer, scanning down a scroll.

"There he is," said Ren, peering over the man's shoulder. "Li San."

"Right," said the registrar, ticking off the name. "Here's your number. Next!"

So Hu had become his father for the day. He laughed. He didn't think Li San would mind. Especially if it gave Hu a chance to go in the competition.

And suddenly Hu realized that Ren had actually done something to help him without being asked. Sometimes, he thought, Ren was as unpredictable as autumn weather. "Hey, thanks," he said.

Ren just shrugged.

"And you?" the officer demanded of Ren.

"I'm new to Company Number Eleven," he said.

"I need your name, then."

"Ren Won," Hu chipped in.

Ren rolled his eyes at him.

The harassed registrar handed over a wooden number tag without even looking up.

The drums rolled again. An officer with a scarred face walked to the front of the pavilion and announced the rules.

"Five shots each per round." His voice carried over the crowd.

"That's First Deputy," said Ren. "He's one of the best

shots in the battalion. It's a good thing he's judging, not competing."

"Outer black circle is ten points," First Deputy continued. "Inner black circle is twenty, red bull's-eye scores fifty. The thirty highest-scoring archers go through to the second and final round."

The soldiers and townspeople around Hu got ready. Some strung their bows, bending the wooden arms to hook the bowstring on. Others trimmed the feathers on their arrows, or squinted down the arrow shafts, doing last-minute checks for cracks and warps. Hu ran his hand over the curves of his weapon. Now that it was fixed, it was as sleek and powerful as Ren's, although it was still colorful. They would have to share Ren's arrows, though — only they were good enough to compete with.

The drums called for the start of the first round. The first set of archers took their places on the line, one in front of each target. They drew arrows from their quivers and set them to the string. Then slowly each man began to draw back his bow. They waited for the signal to shoot.

A sudden movement in the field caught Hu's eye. "Did you see that?"

"What?"

"That flash of gold, out there past the targets."

"No."

"You know, I saw a tiger near the Wall in early summer," Hu told him. "Maybe it's the same one."

"You're seeing things," said Ren.

That's what being hungry does to you, Hu thought.

Dong! A single gong note echoed down the river valley.

Zing! The bowstrings hummed.

Thwack! Thirty arrows hit the straw bales.

Dong! Thwack! On it went, over and over, five shots per man. There seemed to be hundreds of archers.

"So the maximum score is two hundred and fifty," Ren said. "The best archers are scoring in the high one-hundreds."

"Doesn't leave much room for mistakes," said Hu.

Ren shook his head. "Definitely no 'trial and errow' today," he said. "Or we lose."

REN

"Numbers two-hundred-and-ninety to three-hundred-and-seventeen," the registrar called. "Last competitors for the first round."

"That's us!" said Ren and Hu together. They picked up their bows and their quiver of arrows and headed down to the scorched line in the field.

"Take your positions," yelled First Deputy. Ren stayed at the far end of the line, away from the pavilion. He didn't want the deputy seeing him at close quarters. Hu stood beside him, at the next target along.

Ren's heart thumped, but it was a good feeling. He was here with the men, lined up as their equal. And with Hu. They were in it together.

"Good luck," he said to Hu, passing him an arrow from the quiver.

Hu winked at him. *Legendary archer Yi fits an arrow to his bow . . ."* he sang.

"Shut up and concentrate," Ren hissed at him.

"This is how I concentrate," said Hu. "Good luck to you too!"

Ren nocked the arrow on his bow. He stood firm, feet apart, and leaned his hand into the bow's smooth wood, fingers loose. *Don't grip*, he told himself. *The power's in the bow. Let it do its work.*

All along the row, the archers sighted their targets. Silently they drew the bowstrings back to their cheeks. They paused, elbows high, strings tight, muscles tensed.

Dong!

The arrows flew.

Thwack!

Ren's arrow hit the straw bale. It was inside the circle, but only the black one—the outer circle. Ten points. He swore under his breath and looked across to Hu's target. Same score.

"It's the wind," said Hu. "It always gets stronger in the afternoon this time of year."

Ren handed him a second arrow and took one for himself. This time they had to do better.

"Another arrow, please," said Hu. "This one's cracked."

"What?" The arrows had been fine yesterday.

"It's no good."

"It must have gotten damaged in the crush while we were trying to register."

Ren hurried to pass Hu another one and draw his own bow. The rest of the line were ready to shoot.

The gong rang. The second volley of arrows sailed toward the targets. Yes! On the red—fifty points! Now he had a chance. Hu had done better too—twenty points this time. There was just one problem.

"There aren't enough arrows," Ren said urgently to Hu. "There were only ten in the quiver. One's broken, so we're one short."

"Borrow one from someone else?" said Hu.

"Not enough time!" Ren handed him a third arrow.

"Best of four shots gets the fifth arrow," Hu suggested. "That's fair." It was fair. More than fair. Ren was on sixty; Hu had scored only thirty. So far, Ren was in front.

Ren fitted his third arrow to the bow. The gong rang, and he let fly.

The wind shifted it slightly to the right. Twenty points. Curse the wind.

Ren checked Hu's target: bull's-eye. So now they were even. Eighty points each.

He took the fourth arrows out of the quiver. Only one remained. He had to get a bull's-eye to go into the second round. *You can do it,* he said to himself. *To show Master Wang. To show my father.*

Dong! Thwack!

No. He must be looking at the wrong arrow.

Ren squinted at the distant target. He'd missed. Not completely, but it wasn't good enough. His arrow was in the inner black circle — only twenty points.

Hu had hit the red again. That made him one hundred and thirty to Ren's hundred. Hu was in the lead.

"Pig's butt!" Ren kicked the ground.

Hu looked at him with pity. "Come on," he said. "We haven't lost yet. Equal shares, remember?" Hu held out his hand for the final arrow.

Ren was so angry with himself he felt like breaking the arrow and throwing it on the ground. But that would be stupid — neither of them could win then. It was one of the hardest things he'd ever done, but he handed the fifth arrow to Hu.

"It's got to be a bull's-eye," said Ren desperately. "Or we lose."

"I know," said Hu. "Now *you* shut up. So I can concentrate. *The archer takes aim,*" Hu sang softly. He drew his bowstring steadily along the line of his arm, across his cheek to his jaw. *"One unswerving arrow . . ."*

Dong! The gong rang. The line of archers loosed their final shot.

Hu's bowstring hummed. His arrow went swift and straight. *Thwack!* It quivered in the straw bale. Right in the center of the red. Another bull's-eye — they would be through to the second round!

Suddenly an unearthly howl echoed around the river valley. It was long and piercing, like a wild animal. People looked around in panic. Ren saw the cook hustle Lien inside the tent. Several archers reached for new arrows. The Commander and his officers came out of the pavilion and drew their swords.

Then someone spied a golden shape lying on the edge of the field beyond the targets. The Commander strode across the tournament ground toward it. A squad of guards followed him with arrows on their bowstrings and spears leveled.

HU

The tournament was postponed, to be continued at some unknown time in the future. First Deputy came back from the far side of the field to make the announcement, but he didn't say why. Everyone knew it had something to do with that chilling howl and the golden shape on the ground.

As soon as they heard the announcement, Ren got very edgy.

"I have to go," he said, and bolted off through the crowd.

"Wait!" called Hu. He needed the mustache and Mei's trousers back.

But Ren ignored him. He disappeared through the crowd of people making their way back toward the town.

Hu was sure he'd seen a tiger—both behind the competition targets and that summer day outside the Wall. But whatever had been shot was wrapped in sacks and hustled away by the Commander's guards.

Early the next day, an express messenger cantered through the market, sending chickens, geese, and rubbish flying. He galloped out of the main gate and disappeared down the river road like a gust of autumn wind. Another messenger went galloping off to the Wall. Something was going on, but nobody explained what it was to the people of Beicheng, and Hu hadn't spoken to Ren since the day of the festival. A few days later a pair of officers came down to the market area. Magistrate Ding and two soldiers were with them. They looked toward the Lis' house.

"Not Big Ears again," groaned Hu.

"Shh!" said Mei. "Tell Ma to get five bowls of noodles ready, just in case. With eggs, and don't water down the broth. Quick."

Hu passed the instructions inside to his mother and Ah-po and came straight back out to see what was happening.

The officials had stopped in the middle of the market. Hu and Mei couldn't hear what they were saying, but the Magistrate was pointing, sweeping his long sleeves through the air. The officers nodded briefly, then strode straight toward the noodle stall, followed by the soldiers.

"Your Excellencies," Mei said, "we're honored by your visit. If you can wait a few moments, we'd be pleased to serve you."

Big Ears looked hopeful. "They're very good noodles, sir," he said to one of the officers.

"We're not here to eat," said the officer — Hu recognized him as one of the men Ren had hidden from in the toilet. He gestured to the soldiers, who shoved the Lis' door curtain aside with their spears. The officers stepped inside. Hu and Mei didn't dare crowd in after them, but through the doorway they saw their mother stand up from stoking the *kang*. Her face was pale beneath streaks of soot.

Ah-po struggled to her feet too. Both women bowed low.

The officers looked around the little room. Their eyes took in the costume basket and the strings of noodles curled on the kneading board. They seemed to be looking for something. Hu wondered what it could be. One of the officers walked up to the painted bow hanging on the back wall and stared at it.

Did they think it was one of the battalion's? thought Hu. Were they looking for the one he'd gotten with the document from Ren? Perhaps they were in trouble over the army bow. Perhaps that was why Ren was always afraid of being seen. And perhaps Ren's absence had something to do with this visit by the soldiers. Hu went cold with fear and doubt. What had Ren gotten him into?

"By order of Commander Zheng..." said Magistrate Ding. Hu's heart thumped. "We are inspecting Beicheng's defenses. Your hut is built against the town wall."

"Yes, sir," said Ma.

So that was it, thought Hu, relieved.

"It will have to be demolished," said the officer.

Hu was shocked. His mother held one hand over her mouth. Mei gasped. Ah-po rocked back and forth, moaning.

"Sirs, we have nowhere else to live," Ma pleaded.

"Won't you have a bowl of noodles and reconsider?" Mei said.

"Beicheng is under threat," said the officer. "We must make sure the town's defenses will hold against attack."

"Permission to check the outside of the walls and the gates, Second Deputy?" said his comrade.

Second Deputy nodded curtly, and they all left without having any noodles. The Li family sat down in stunned silence. Hu thought of the bad sticks he'd thrown—the north snake and darkness—and wondered if they were coming true.

"Magistrate Ding might persuade them to leave it here," said Mei. "He won't get any rent if it's knocked down."

"We've got no money to rent anywhere else," Ma said. "I wish your father was here." But Li San was still working on the Wall. And since the soldiers had told Hu not to come back, he couldn't even tell his father what was happening.

Hu slipped out of their house to watch the soldiers from a wary distance. The men took the makeshift ladder from above the toilet and broke it. He heard them hacking the toilet roof apart so no one could climb up from the other side. This was what they'd do to his home, Hu realized. His family's shelter and security were to be ripped away, just before winter set in. Hu might not be in trouble over the bow, but this was just as bad.

REN

After the archery competition had been postponed, Commander Zheng had issued a series of orders. He'd had the top level of the town hall tower re-opened and stationed a full-time watch up there. He'd sent an express messenger out of Beicheng on one of his best horses, and ordered that the men on the Wall work an extra shift.

Ren looked for an opportunity to ask his father what had interrupted the competition and when the finals would be held. But for several days the Commander had been too busy to approach.

Ren was stuck in the town hall. He couldn't climb out over the roofs to meet Hu without being seen by the guards above. He hid the bow and the borrowed armor at the bottom of his clothes chest. Then, because he had nothing better to do, he tackled Chapter Two of *Mathematical Techniques*.

Master Wang entered the study, cracking his knuckles. Ren thought he looked pleased about something. Ren dreaded to think what that might be. Maybe he'd found something particularly worthy and boring for Ren to learn.

Ren and his tutor bowed at each other, stiff with mutual dislike.

"*Master* Ren," the tutor sneered. "Unfortunately your education is to be temporarily suspended."

Ren's heart leaped.

"The Commander has seen fit to send me on an important assignment. It is a matter of pressing business. I am going to the provincial city of Wuzhong to complete an investigation."

Master Wang was going away! What a relief. Maybe his father had changed his mind. Perhaps he realized Ren had suffered enough. Maybe Second Deputy could take him on for a while as an assistant. At worst, Ren might be left with Lien in the care of the cook, who was an old softy and would let them get away with anything.

Master Wang smiled. "To such a *promising* student," he continued sarcastically, "lack of teaching will make little difference. Your father wishes to speak to you in his study."

Ren felt immensely hopeful as he hurried downstairs.

In the Commander's study, a half-written letter and the Commander's seal lay on the low writing table. Beside it was a long piece of tiger skin, with stripes as dark as night. Ren wondered what it was doing there. He'd never seen it before. Commander Zheng was pacing up and down the room. He didn't look at his son. Ren thought with a shiver of apprehension that he did not look like someone about to give good news.

"Ah, Ren," said Commander Zheng. "I didn't intend this to happen, but it's the only way."

"What is, sir?" Ren asked in alarm. Had his father found out about his rooftop escapes? Or, even worse, did he know about the faked order for the bow? He could have sworn he'd wiped the seal clean, but maybe his father was suspicious. Had Master Wang told on him?

"You know that I had to stop the archery competition?" the Commander said.

Ren nodded. Had his father seen him shooting? Was that what this was about?

"What you don't know, because I didn't have it announced, is the reason why. One of the archers in the competition shot a wide arrow, which hit something in the long grass beyond the targets. You might have heard the scream."

Ren remembered what Hu had said about the tiger and looked at the skin on the floor. Did that have anything to do with it? His father followed his eyes.

"Magnificent, isn't it? But, no, it wasn't an animal that he shot. It was a man. A barbarian spy."

Ren breathed in sharply. "What happened to him?" He said.

"Don't ask," said the Commander with a grimace. "The skin was part of his clothing. A mark of high rank." Commander Zheng frowned and began to pace up and down the room again. "For the barbarians to send one of their nobles inside the Wall, secretly, means something big is happening out there to the north. The horsemen's army is on the move. Now, I'm under orders from the Emperor not to attack. I can't do anything to break the truce that he made with the barbarians."

"Sir!" First Deputy came in. He bowed to the Commander and nodded curtly to Ren. The old scar on the officer's face made the corner of his mouth turn down in a permanent grimace. Ren felt uncomfortable, remembering the injury he'd caused.

"The boat will be ready at first light tomorrow," First Deputy said. "They will go via Wuzhong."

"Good," replied the Commander. "Tell Master Wang to be ready. Ren, you will go with him. You will return to the capital."

"Me?" Ren exclaimed. "Go with Master Wang? Back home?" The thought nearly made him choke.

"Yes," said the Commander. He hooked his thumbs into his belt.

"I hate Master Wang," Ren said. "He's poisonous. Please, sir, not back to the capital!" Both Commander Zheng and First Deputy were frowning, but Ren pressed on. He was desperate. "I promise to behave if you let me stay."

"Master Wang is very clever and very capable," said the Commander sternly. "You don't like him because he disciplines you, but that is exactly what you need. You will do as you're told. Even a Commander must follow orders." He turned to First Deputy. "The Emperor's reply can't be expected to arrive until full moon. The extra troops we need will take seven or eight days longer—that's close on a month. The barbarians probably know the Wall repairs aren't finished. They'll want to take advantage of that. We can't be sure how long we've got, so we have to assume the worst.

"Ren—you will leave. I don't know if . . . when I will see you again. Look after your little sister. I am sorry it has come to this."

Ren was devastated. His father was sending him away. He might never see him again. And he and Lien were being given into the clutches of Master Wang.

HU

The market was full of rumors: the Magistrate was leaving; the Emperor was coming; the Emperor wasn't coming; the barbarians were.

The town had to get ready, but most people did not know for what. Big Ears told Mei to watch for a red flag going up at the watchtower during the day or fire there at night. He said that meant "they" were coming. He didn't know when the Lis' house would be pulled down.

Then the Li family was low on flour again, so Big Ears and Rat's Teeth stopped coming to the stall.

"We don't have enough money to buy more flour at that ridiculous price," sighed Ma after counting their short string of copper coins.

"Maybe we could sell something to get cash," Mei suggested.

Ma shook her head. "I don't know what," she said. "I don't want to sell our warm clothes with winter coming. I can't sell the cooking pots, or how will we make a living? And who's going to want props and costumes at a time like this?"

She looked around the room. Her gaze stopped on the wall opposite.

Hu saw what she was looking at. "No!" he exclaimed. "Not that! You can't sell our bow. The tournament's not finished yet. I made it into the final round. Please!"

"Hu, we have to eat." His mother's voice was sharp. Hu hated it when worry made her bad-tempered. "We can live without the weapon, whatever you think. We should get a good price for it with all these soldiers around."

"But the competition's our best chance! I could win."

Ma twisted the string of coins tightly together.

"One day soon you may wish you'd never seen a bow. Enough!" she said as Hu opened his mouth to protest.

The decision was made. Hu dragged behind Mei to the marketplace.

His mother was right about the price. Mei haggled patiently with the secondhand dealer for nearly an hour while Hu looked on in stony silence. Eventually Mei got enough money to buy flour for the whole winter. Hu could hardly bear to look at the coins. All his efforts had been reduced to this—a few copper pieces jingling on a string. The competition would come and go without him. The coins would get used up too, and then they'd be back with nothing. He wished his mother could see that, but she wouldn't listen.

"Maybe you can borrow a bow from somebody if the tournament ever happens," Mei said.

"Yeah, like the vegetable seller's warped and splintery piece of rubbish?" said Hu bitterly. "You just sold Archer Yi's weapon. It was beautiful."

Mei tucked the money inside her jacket and put an arm over Hu's shoulders. "Sometimes poor people just have to put up with things," she said.

He shrugged her arm off.

"Why?" he demanded. "Only old women like Ah-po say stuff like that." Hu didn't care if he offended her. He wanted to get away and be by himself. "I'm not going to get flour," he said. "I don't want to."

Hu couldn't go up to the Wall because it was swarming with soldiers. He headed for the river instead. He sat on the yellow cliffs and watched the water swirl below, muddy as his thoughts. Dusk began to fall. Upstream, somebody was loading a barge by the riverbank. *Funny time to do it in the dark,* Hu thought. Nothing was the way it used to be in Beicheng.

The arrival of the Emperor's troops had been like a legend come to life. The battalion's arrival and training for the competition had given him new hope. But now Ren was keeping away and the army had taken his father, their food, and soon even their home. And his hopes had been sold along with the family's bow—gone, like a bowl of spilled soup.

REN

Ren's trip downriver to Wuzhong was cold and depressing. Most of Ren's life had been depressing, he thought, but this was the worst yet. Every oar-stroke took him closer to his father's First Wife and the capital, and farther away from the Commander and the battalion. But there was no going back—his father had rejected him.

Ren didn't like traveling by boat. The barge was very low in the water, and the wind slapped the river against its flat sides, too close for comfort. He had only Master Wang; Lien; a tall, clumsy guard with big ears; and a boatman to distract him from his unhappiness.

Ren had nothing to do for three days except sit on his clothes chest and watch the scenery go by: cliffs, fields, hills, sheep, and huts, and more hills, sheep, and huts. He tried to keep behind the cargo, out of the wind and Master Wang's sight, in case the tutor thought of some punishment for him. After all, there was plenty Ren could be punished for. But Master Wang stayed under cover; he read his scrolls and added up lists with his abacus. Lien played with her dolls. The guard didn't have much to say.

To pass the time, Ren pretended he was shooting the sheep along the bank. His bow and the quiver of arrows were still safely stowed in his chest, unknown to anyone else.

Ren wished he could use them. He wished he and Hu had won the competition.

But it was too late now—there wouldn't be any competition. The barbarians were like an unseen flood rising on the far side of the Wall. The Commander was not sure he could defeat them. Could they swallow up Beicheng and the battalion as easily as the river could swamp the boat? Ren hoped the extra troops from the capital would reach Beicheng in time.

Ren wondered what might happen to Hu. Would he ever see him again? If he were here, Hu would probably tell dumb jokes, and Ren would have someone to argue with. Someone who was almost his equal, in a way he couldn't quite explain. Equal in age, at least, not little like Lien or old and mean like Master Wang. Ren missed Hu.

Finally, on the third afternoon, the barge passed through another set of yellow cliffs, around another corner, and there was Wuzhong. It was a walled town like Beicheng, only bigger. The flags of a different battalion were flying from its gates. There was a lot of traffic in and out.

Master Wang made Ren and Lien stand behind him as the barge pulled in slowly to the wharf. "I have a letter of introduction to the local government from Commander Zheng," he told them. "Wuzhong is the main city of this province. Under the enlightened legal system of our ancestors, this is where government records for this area are kept. Including the criminal records." Master Wang rubbed his hands together. "Ah, I look forward to dealing with civilized people again."

"What do you need the criminal records for?" Ren asked.

Master Wang gave him a withering look. Ren wished he'd kept his mouth shut.

"Ah. How little you understand. Possibly less than I'd thought," the tutor mused.

As the barge docked, Master Wang gave a scroll to the tall guard. "Present this at the gate," he told him.

The guard did as he was instructed, and before long a pair of carriages arrived at the wharf. Two men in long black robes dismounted. Master Wang, Ren, and Lien climbed ashore and greeted them.

"Welcome, honorable Master Wang. You've had a hard trip?"

"No, no, thank you, thank you," Master Wang's sleeves almost swept the ground as he bowed.

The formalities between the adults went on and on while the luggage was unloaded from the barge. Ren had forgotten how stuffy government officials were. The officials told Master Wang the latest news from the capital and tutted over the grain shortage. They all tried to work out which of the three knew the most important people. The politeness seemed to last forever.

"Excuse me," said Lien. Master Wang frowned. Girls weren't supposed to talk in the presence of strange men. Ren pinched her so she would be quiet.

"Commander Zheng will soon be expecting a messenger from the Emperor," Master Wang was saying. "He should pass through Wuzhong on the way to Beicheng. Can you inform me when that happens?"

"We would be pleased to acquaint you with the Master of the Postal Service," one of the officials replied.

"Indeed, indeed," said Master Wang. "I am honored." He tucked his hands inside his sleeves. "Perhaps as a great favor . . ." he paused, jingling the coin purse kept in his sleeve, "you might also introduce me to some eminent people in the grain business?"

"Certainly, certainly."

Lien could not stop herself any longer and began to chatter. "Don't you know?" she said to Master Wang. "There's lots of grain on the boat."

"My *dear* miss," said the tutor, "a girl like you doesn't know very much. Of course there isn't grain on the barge. How could there be?" He narrowed his eyes and gave a high-pitched laugh, as if to say how silly she was.

Lien didn't smile back. Ren didn't blame her.

"Beicheng doesn't have any grain to spare." The tutor cracked his knuckles and looked down at the little girl. "That's why I'm here in Wuzhong, of course."

The Wuzhong officials nodded their understanding. Ignoring Lien, they ushered Master Wang into the first carriage. The soldier helped Ren and his sister into the second carriage.

"Ren," said Lien, looking earnestly into his face, "there *was* grain on the boat. Master Wang wasn't telling the truth."

"Rubbish," said Ren. "Master Wang is an odious cockroach. All officials are. But Beicheng doesn't have any grain to send here."

"Look," said Lien. "My dollies were playing banquets." She took a tiny toy pot out of her sleeve. She tipped the pot up in her palm, and held out her hand to Ren. Half a dozen millet grains were heaped in Lien's hand. "There was a little hole in one of the sacks on the boat," she explained.

"Funny," said Ren.

"I was right, wasn't I?"

"Yes, you were," Ren said. "But don't say anything more to Master Wang, or he'll just make fun of you."

"Nasty Master Wang," she said.

"Shh," warned Ren, in case the soldier was listening.

Something was niggling in the back of his mind. Bits of

information were clicking into place like abacus beads. Ren was getting the measure of Master Wang, he thought. He knew for certain that his tutor was lying, and that he was somehow responsible for the missing grain. At the time of the autumn downpour, Ren had agreed to keep quiet, in return for Master Wang's silence about Ren's own misdeeds. Now, perhaps, the tutor had convinced the Commander to have Ren sent away. Master Wang was cunning. Because what good was Ren's knowledge in a strange city, where he knew no one? He and Lien were completely in the tutor's hands.

HU

After selling the bow, the Li family found that there was no flour to buy at any price. The soldiers wouldn't even let Mei into the grain store, she said, and the grain seller looked very unhappy. All Hu's mother could get for her string of cash was a sack of turnips and a pile of cabbages from the vegetable seller. Hu was even hungrier now. The first frost came, and still he had not seen Ren.

"The Commander's family has gone," Mei said, when Hu got back from collecting firewood one day.

"Have they?" said Hu. "How do you know?"

He was surprised. Why hadn't Ren come to tell him first? What if Ren never came back? He still had Mei's trousers. And the only bow. Yet somehow Hu felt he had lost even more than those things. Hu had come to think of Ren as a friend—someone who shared his brightest dream.

"That little girl who used to visit the market with their cook stopped coming," Mei said. "When I asked the cook if she was sick, he told me she and her brother both went back to the capital. It's too dangerous here, he said."

"If Beicheng's too dangerous for them, what about us?" Hu protested. So he'd been wrong about Ren. The nobleman's son had run off back to the capital at the first hint of danger. Hu's stomach growled angrily.

"Ma, maybe we should leave too," Mei said.

"Not while your father's working on the Wall and we still have a home to live in," Ma said.

Hu was relieved. He didn't want to leave his father. They had nothing but each other now.

The vegetable seller put his head around the Lis' door.

"There are soldiers coming," he said. "They're asking for you!"

"*Aiya, aiya!*" moaned Ah-po. "Heaven protect us! Things are getting worse, as sure as the river flows."

"Don't get upset, Ah-po," said Ma. "We'll manage." But her face looked pale.

Hu didn't know how they would manage with no house in the freezing depths of winter.

The vegetable seller disappeared suddenly from the door frame. A spear ripped through the door curtain, and half a dozen soldiers burst into the room.

Hu and Mei huddled together against the wall. Ma dropped to her knees and bowed with her face to the ground.

"In the name of His Imperial Majesty, ruler of the Han Kingdom," shouted a soldier, "where is Li San?"

"If it please you, my lords," Hu's mother answered in a shaky voice, "he is working for the Emperor on the Great Wall."

The soldier glared at the family suspiciously.

"Who are you?" demanded the soldier.

"His wife, sir."

"Don't bother with the women," interrupted another soldier. "Who's the boy?"

"My son," Ma said.

"Take him!" ordered the soldier. Two men stepped forward and grabbed Hu by the elbows.

"Move!" barked one of them, kneeing him in the back.

"Please don't hurt him, sir," Ma begged. "My son's done nothing wrong."

"Yes, he has. We are arresting him for theft." The soldier turned away. "We'll be back tomorrow to knock down the house."

Then the men shoved Hu out the door. As he tripped over the threshold, he heard someone sob behind him. He turned to look, to say something to his family, but a soldier cuffed him over the head. His feet stumbled forward while his brain struggled to make sense of what was happening.

The soldiers marched Hu through the marketplace. All the Lis' neighbors, people Hu had known all his life, stared at him with fear in their faces. The secondhand dealer and the wine merchant turned their backs. Nobody greeted him. It was the same look, Hu remembered, that the gambling soldiers at the Wall had given him. *The north snake and darkness. . . . Clear out before you bring bad luck on all of us. . . .*

Maybe I am cursed, he thought.

The guards hustled Hu up through the town to the town hall. An image of Ren flashed briefly through his mind. Perhaps his friend would be able to help him. But no, he wasn't even in Beicheng anymore.

The soldiers rapped on the gate with a spear.

A guard opened up as soon as he saw them, as if he was expecting them.

"Over there," said the guard, pointing to a heavily barred door leading off the courtyard.

The soldiers pulled the bolts, opened the door, and pushed Hu in. He fell on the floor. The bolts squealed shut behind him. He was imprisoned.

It was a tiny room. Shadows clogged the corners. Something smelled. There was one small window high up—too small for Hu to climb through, even if he could reach. Why should he escape anyway? Where could he go? What had he done wrong? Why was he here? Did it have to do with their house? Did it have to do with Ren?

Day turned into night as Hu shivered miserably. Soldiers changed shift outside, but no one opened the door to Hu's prison.

Through the small window Hu saw the moon come out. The wind pushed wisps of cloud across her face. The clouds tumbled away as if they were frightened. Hu thought of Archer Yi's wife, the Lady of the Moon. That reminded him of his mother—her face shocked and white when the soldiers had come. Hu had never spent a night away from his family; he felt he was being swallowed up by loneliness. He wrapped his arms around his legs, hid his face in his knees, and cried.

He stayed like that a long time, while the distant moon watched. Something inside him was turning into cold, hard stone. His heart was frozen, and he couldn't move. He drifted into half sleep. Nightmares stalked his thoughts—creeping, gathering, preparing to pounce.

In the middle of the night, something hit him on the head. He cried out in alarm and opened his eyes. A pebble gleamed faintly on the floor.

"Shh!" came a voice from outside. "It's me—Mei."

"What?" No one but the moon was in sight.

There was no answer. But something came sailing through the window and landed on the floor with a thud.

It was a turnip. Purple-gray in the moonlight, but better than solid gold to Hu.

Another dark shape flashed past the moon and missed the window.

"Darn," said Mei in a hoarse whisper. Next time the missile came through the small gap and Hu caught it in both hands. It was a bun. Small, but warm, wrapped in a rag. She must have heated it on the *kang* at home. His mother had used the last of their flour to make a bun for him.

"Thank you," he croaked.

"I know it wasn't you," Mei whispered.

"Quick, go!" said Hu. "Or they might put you in here too."

"I'll be all right. Don't worry. Bye!" Then she was gone.

Hu thought he might have imagined her or been talking to a ghost. But the bun was hot in his hands and smelled of home. And the turnip was . . . well, like every other turnip his family had eaten in recent days. He chewed slowly, savoring every mouthful.

REN

Cooped up in the Wuzhong guesthouse, Ren worked through the entire third chapter of *Mathematical Techniques*. It gave him something to do. It also stopped him from thinking too much about his father in Beicheng. Or about going back to the capital. This was what he'd learned to do after his mother had died—forget everything.

Master Wang, however, was looking very pleased with himself.

"When will we leave?" Lien whined. "I'm tired of here. I want to go home."

"Good girls don't complain," the tutor scolded. "Nevertheless, I think it won't be too long now, Miss Lien. My first task is done. I have identified a likely suspect in the criminal records for the theft of the grain supplies."

"What?" Ren asked, looking up from his scroll. "Who?"

"A person of no importance," sniffed Master Wang. "A culprit with a history of stealing."

"Are you going to tell my father?" Ren asked.

"Of course," said Master Wang. "I have already sent an express messenger. He should be there by now."

So that was the tutor's scheme. Master Wang was going to shift the blame for the missing grain onto somebody else. He would completely fool the Commander, and Ren couldn't stop him.

The tutor rubbed his hands and cracked his knuckles in expectation. His mouth pinched into a tight smile. He looked like a predator stalking prey, but not with Ren in his sights this time.

"There is one further matter I have not quite taken care of," Master Wang said. "Remain here." He pointed to the floor with a curved fingernail. "Or you'll regret it."

Ren did as he was told. There was nothing else he could do.

"Play with me, Big Brother. I'm bored." Lien was arranging banquets with her dolls again.

Ren wasn't interested in stuff like that, especially not now. He was angry that Master Wang seemed to be getting away with his devious plans. If he could only prove to the Commander that Master Wang was a liar, then the Commander wouldn't believe any accusations against Ren, either. Perhaps he would take his son back. What Ren needed was evidence. More evidence than Lien's sprinkle of grain in a doll's pot.

An idea formed in his mind. *If there's one thing I am good at,* Ren thought, *it's adding up, after all those chapters of math.* There was something he wanted to try—and this time it wasn't escaping.

"Lien," Ren said, "remember what we talked about in the carriage when we arrived here? The grain on the boat and Master Wang being nasty?"

"Yes." She nodded.

"I'm going to find out what's going on. Whatever you do, don't tell Master Wang what I'm doing, or we'll both be in trouble." More trouble, if that was possible.

"Ooh," she said with wide, teary eyes. "Don't be naughty, Ren."

"Don't cry," he said impatiently. "I'm not doing anything naughty. Just . . . um, math homework."

"Oh," said Lien, losing interest. She went back to her dolls.

Ren examined the tutor's travel chest. It was locked. Stupid thing. He searched around the room for something to open it with. He took off his belt buckle and pared down one of the bamboo strips from his homework scroll. He put the sharp point into the lock.

The strip broke. Ren started again on another homework strip. This time he didn't scrape the bamboo quite so thin, and when he tried it on the chest, something moved inside. After a bit of fiddling, the lock was open. Ren lifted the lid.

A pair of spare shoes and a thick winter gown lay on top. Boring black, of course, like everything the tutor wore, and very tidy. Ren felt uneasy. Poking around in Master Wang's possessions was a lot like being a rabbit sniffing around in a fox's hole.

Ren was looking for a scroll, not clothes, so he dug deeper. He picked up the gown to move it aside and discovered it was surprisingly heavy. As the sleeves unfolded, Ren heard a distinct clink. He shook the coat. It jingled. Ren lay the gown on the floor and looked inside it. As well as the usual wads of silk padding for warmth, the lining seemed to have rows of flat, round lumps in it. Ren picked at one of them with his sharpened stick. A gold coin glinted at him through the silk threads.

Ren was surprised. He hadn't expected this. If Master Wang had been wealthy, he wouldn't have gone to Beicheng, a place he detested, just to be a supply secretary. And clearly the tutor wanted to keep the coins hidden. The money must have come from selling the stolen grain.

Ren pushed the heavy coat aside and returned to the chest. He sighed. There was a bamboo scroll in there all right—a whole box full of them.

He didn't know where to start, so he began on the left and worked toward the right. There was stuff by Confucius: *The Spring and Autumn Annals* and the *Analects*. Then something called *Records of the Grand Historian*, and *Mathematical Techniques Chapters Five through Nine*, and on it went. He sped up. The pile of scrolls on the floor got higher. *Rules Governing the Imperial Armory, Rules for Military Reports*, then, in Master Wang's handwriting, a record of arrows issued to troops in Beicheng.

Uh-oh, Ren thought. If he had time he'd read that one later, to see if it said anything about the quiverful issued to Hu.

Aha. This might be what he was after: a record of grain received in Beicheng. Another record, this one of grain stored in Beicheng. Another list of grain stored in Beicheng. *Why bother having two of the same thing?* Ren thought. Master Wang was obsessed with these stupid bits of bamboo. Yet another one—a record of grain used in Beicheng.

Ren unrolled the first grain scroll. *"Four hundred measures received by river on the fifteenth day of the seventh month,"* he read.

Ren didn't know or care much about grain normally. It was something for peasants and the cook and boring people like Master Wang to worry about. But he'd seen the huge baskets used for measuring. Four hundred measures was a lot of grain. Enough to feed the battalion for months, he guessed. And there was more. *"Two hundred measures by barge on the twelfth day of the ninth month."* That was in the battalion's early days in Beicheng. Ren had seen the barges being unloaded.

Ren got out his brush and his homework scroll, and started adding. After a couple of hours of scribbling, re-adding and double-checking, he worked out the totals for all three grain lists: Six hundred and twenty measures of army grain supplies had arrived in Beicheng over the summer. Two hundred and five measures had been given out as rations to soldiers and workers, up until Master Wang left the town. Only one hundred and fifteen measures remained in the Beicheng grain store.

Ren wrote himself a summary, just to be sure:

    620 (supplied)

    –205 (used)

    <u>–115 (left)</u>

    300 (?)

So that meant there really was grain missing. Three hundred measures of it.

Most interesting of all, Master Wang's second record of "grain stored" was not the same as the first one. In it there were exactly three hundred measures listed against the word *ding*.

Ding meant "nail." What did nails have to do with grain supplies? Had Master Wang accidentally mixed up the supply lists?

He reread the scroll. The way the list was set out, it looked as if "Nail" was the place where the millet was stored.

"The Magistrate! Magistrate Ding. That's it!" Ren shouted. Lien stopped playing with her dolls and looked up in surprise. "That's where the missing grain went. His house is right next door to the grain store. They *were* stealing, and they've brought it here to sell. The sneaky, creepy, poisonous, skulking—"

"Ren! Ren!" Lien twittered like a little bird that had seen a snake. Ren froze.

"*So,*" came Master Wang's cold voice from the doorway. "I see you have been busy while I've been away."

HU

After a night in prison, Hu was relieved to hear the bolts being opened. By now someone would surely have realized that they'd made a mistake, and they'd come to set him free.

A guard threw the door open with a bang.

"Get up, scum," he said. A pair of soldiers dragged and pushed Hu out into the courtyard. Magistrate Ding, wearing his official seal around his neck, sat in front of a writing table. Rat's Teeth was there, and several other soldiers.

A man was kneeling in the middle of the courtyard. He faced the Magistrate with his back to Hu. His head was bowed and his shoulders slumped. The man's hands were tied tightly behind his back. Hu noticed the hands were wide and brown and chapped from hard work. Then with a shock Hu recognized them. They were his father's hands.

Magistrate Ding was sitting in the same place as he had for the banquet months ago. Hu and his father were going to be center stage this time too, he realized. Only it wasn't for a performance of Archer Yi's story.

"Li San," said Magistrate Ding. "Resident of Beicheng, performer and noodle seller."

"Sir," croaked Hu's father.

"Li Hu," Magistrate Ding said. "Son of Li San."

"Kneel!" ordered the soldier, shoving Hu forward.

Hu fell on his knees. The soldier twisted his arms up

behind him and tied his hands with a rope. Hu's father looked sideways at him. His face was bruised, and his eyes were black and sad as death. Hu felt sick.

"You are accused of stealing imperial grain supplies from the Beicheng grain store," the Magistrate said harshly. "Confess!"

"I didn't do it, sir," Li San answered. "Nor my son, either. We're honest people. We have nothing to do with this."

"Boy?"

Hu didn't know what to say. He didn't understand what was going on. He shook his head.

"Where is the missing grain?" demanded the Magistrate.

"I don't know, sir. I don't know about any grain. My family is poor. We don't have it," said Li San.

Magistrate Ding turned to an officer. Hu recognized him as one of the men who had come to their home the day before.

"What did you find when you searched the house?"

"A string of cash," said the officer, passing it to the Magistrate. Hu wanted to grab it off him — it was all that was left over from selling the bow and all the money his family had. "Along with a handful of flour, a couple of old costumes, and a sack of turnips. No grain to speak of, but there were these." The soldier held up a pair of trousers. The black silk rippled like a flag. They were Ren's. Hu swallowed. No ordinary family was supposed to own clothes like that. Hu knew it didn't look good. But if that was all they had against him, he could explain.

"They're not ours, sir," Hu told the Magistrate. "They belong to Zheng Ren, the son of the Commander."

"Aha," said Magistrate Ding.

Hu was about to say more, but the Magistrate held up

his hand for silence and the soldier guarding Hu kneed him in the back.

"What other evidence do we have against this family?"

Rat's Teeth stepped forward. *Not you again,* thought Hu. *Always hanging around like a bad smell.*

"If ya please, yer honor. I've got something to add."

"Speak," nodded the Magistrate.

"Right back in summer, I was on duty here 'n I saw this boy. He had a barrow loaded with flour. When I asked his business, this boy assaulted me. Then he ran away with the flour," said Rat's Teeth.

"It was ours," said Hu. "He tried to take it!"

"I wasn't asking you," the Magistrate said sternly. "I was asking him." He gestured at Rat's Teeth. "I see. Any other witnesses?"

Another soldier spoke up. "Excuse me, Magistrate. I didn't think anything of this at the time, but it might be relevant."

"Go on."

"Before the Mid-Autumn Festival, I was on guard outside the hall one night. Just before dawn, I saw this kid hanging around outside the grain store. I challenged him, and he didn't have a good reason for being there. Said he was collecting mushrooms for ghosts or some such."

The soldiers around the courtyard sniggered.

Hu's father looked at him.

"I wasn't stealing," said Hu. "I was meeting a friend — Zheng Ren, who owns the trousers."

The Magistrate and the soldiers looked at him in disbelief.

"Don't you go accusing noble people and dragging them into your bad deeds," the Magistrate warned.

"But it's true," Hu said.

"Quiet!" The soldier behind Hu cuffed him over the ear. The Magistrate called on an officer to speak next.

"Your responsibilities, sir?"

"I supervise the armory, Magistrate."

"Not the grain store?"

"No, Magistrate. But in the ninth month of this year, I issued a bow and quiver to this boy. The order was signed by the Commander, and the weapons were for Company Number Eleven. But the company leader reports he never received the weapons."

"I don't have them," said Hu. *If only Ren was here to explain,* he thought desperately.

"Now will you confess?" the Magistrate said to Li San. "A fox's tail always shows. Bad deeds can't be kept hidden."

"We're an honest family, sir," Hu's father answered. "My son tells the truth."

Hu was deeply grateful to his father. At least *he* believed him.

"An honest family, are you? *Eh-hmm!*" The Magistrate cleared his throat and held up a bamboo scroll. "Listen to this. An express message, which arrived overnight, from the provincial records kept in Wuzhong: *In the year of the Monkey, during the reign of Emperor Shun* — that's eighteen years ago, by my count — *transported to Beicheng, one Li San, convicted for theft of grain.* What do you say to that?"

His father couldn't be a criminal. Hu didn't believe it. They must have the wrong person.

"I don't deny that, sir," Li San answered. "But it was a long time ago, and I've already suffered for it. And I haven't taken anything that wasn't mine, then or now."

Hu felt dizzy. It was the same bad feeling as when an

acrobatic stunt went wrong: the world was upside down; he was out of control and about to get hurt.

"So," said Magistrate Ding, "it is true there's no sign of the missing grain. However, as your family runs a noodle stall, it's all been cooked and eaten, I'd say. There's plenty of other evidence pointing to your guilt. And you have a criminal record. In conclusion, I declare the Li family guilty of stealing Imperial supplies. Count yourselves lucky there's a labor crisis here, or your punishment would be harsher. I sentence you both to three years hard labor."

"No!" said Hu. "You've got it wrong!"

"Keep quiet, boy," Li San whispered urgently. "You'll make it worse."

The Magistrate wrote his decision on the bamboo scroll with a brush and stamped it with his seal. Then he dismissed them with a wave of his hand. The trial was over.

REN

At the inn in Wuzhong, Ren faced his tutor.

"You know what happened to the grain supplies from Beicheng," Ren accused him.

"Certainly," Master Wang replied. "They were stolen by a certain Li San, local resident and convicted criminal."

"That's a lie!" said Ren. He had a feeling he knew the name, but fear and anger ran hot and cold through him, and he couldn't think. "Magistrate Ding had them, and you knew."

"Is that so?" said Master Wang, putting the tips of his fingers together so his long fingernails arched through the air. "Now, how do you know that?"

"It's in those," said Ren, pointing to the scrolls all over the floor. "There are two records, the real one and another one for my father to see," he accused the tutor.

Master Wang picked up the records Ren had been reading and tucked them inside his robe.

"Just *who* will believe *you?*" Master Wang smiled. "You are a disobedient and deceitful child. You break into other people's property," Master Wang waved his fingernails at the opened chest. "In Beicheng you injured an Imperial officer. Then you went out without permission and in the process destroyed a valuable scroll. You associated with vulgar peasants. Not even your father wants you. He's so unimpressed by you, he has sent you away."

Ren flushed bright red. His fists clenched. He didn't know what to say. He felt like a fly struggling as Master Wang wound a web around him. Everything the man had said was true. Ren was as guilty as a convict on the Wall. So was Master Wang, but Ren couldn't prove it without the scrolls.

Lien watched from the corner with both hands over her mouth.

"I have an important matter to attend to," said Master Wang. "I have just had word that an Imperial courier has been sighted, very possibly with new orders for your father from His Imperial Majesty. I will collect that layabout guard from the wineshop downstairs so I can make sure those orders reach the *right* destination." He cackled. "Then we must leave immediately." Master Wang picked his lined coat up from the floor and put it on.

"Perhaps," he said with a scalding smile, "you know rather too much about the missing grain. After all, the disgraced children of a slave girl are of no consequence. They have even less power and influence than a defeated Commander. Grain is not the only profitable trade."

He left, and Lien started to cry. "Ren," she sobbed, "I'm scared!"

A month ago, Ren would have told her not to be a sissy. But she had been right about the grain on the boat. And she was right to be frightened of Master Wang.

"Shh," Ren said. "Let me think and don't fuss."

What was going to happen to them? Whatever Master Wang's plans were, they wouldn't be good. What did he mean about "profitable trade"? A terrible thought dawned on Ren. Children could be sold—in the marketplaces of big towns. If Ren was sold into slavery and the battalion was defeated in battle, Master Wang's tracks would be covered. Nobody would know or care what he'd done. Could Ren run away? He didn't know anyone in Wuzhong. In the capital, his father's First Wife wouldn't take in a runaway, and returning to his father in Beicheng was impossible.

Ren suddenly knew what he could do. He could find Hu and his family. They were poor, but poverty was better than slavery, or whatever else Master Wang had in mind. Hu would help him. If Ren could only get away.

"Listen," Ren said to Lien. "Master Wang hates me, and now that I know about the grain, he hates me even more. I'm going to run away."

"What about me?" said Lien, with tears trickling down her cheeks. "Can I come too?"

Ren hadn't thought about her. "Look after your little sister," his father had said. Master Wang might be planning to sell her as well. He couldn't abandon her. She was too little, and none of this was her fault. That was it! Lien hadn't done anything wrong, so Ren could take her with him to Beicheng, back to the Commander. It was a lot of responsibility; it was dangerous. But it was less dangerous than leaving her to Master Wang.

"All right," Ren said. "You'll need lots of warm clothes," he told her. "But not your best coat, because it's too pretty. We don't want everyone to notice. And we need some pieces of jewelry we can use for money. Hide them under your clothes—you can't parade around like a princess now. You can't take your dolls with you, either."

Lien's lips started to tremble again.

"If you want to keep them," Ren said impatiently, "you

have to stay with Master Wang. If you come with me, you can only take what you can carry. It's your choice."

"I want to come with you, Big Brother." Lien put her hand in his.

"Then do as I say." Her trust made him feel stronger. At least one person wanted him and didn't think he was all bad.

But how could they sneak out of the inn and head back to Beicheng unnoticed? Ren went to his own chest and took out the trousers belonging to Hu's sister, which he'd never had a chance to take back. The false mustache was in there too, and the old armor. Ren put on the same costume he'd worn on the day of the tournament, but this time he wore his own winter clothes underneath. He pasted on the mustache using some mushed-up grains of leftover millet from lunch. Lien watched amazed.

Ren took out the bow and arrows. It felt good to have them in his hands again. He might not be the best shot in Beicheng, but at least he knew how to use them.

"We'll be safe with these," he told Lien. "If the innkeeper asks on the way out, tell him you're going shopping for the trip back to the capital. Don't call me 'Big Brother.' I'm your guard." He winked at her.

"Are we going to the capital?" said Lien.

"No," said Ren. "We're going to find a boat or a horse to take us to Beicheng."

冬

DONG

WINTER

HU

Hu lay on the hard dirt in the cold dark. An iron ring around his neck chained him to a stake in the ground.

Here there was no *kang,* no quilt, no Ma, no Mei. Not even Ah-po's snores to send him off to sleep. Only the ghosts of the Wall for company and his father lying beside him.

But who was Li San anyway? How could his father be a criminal? The iron convict ring was as icy as the fingers of winter around Hu's throat. He curled his knees into his chest.

"Hu?" Li San whispered in the dark.

"Go away," he replied.

"I can't," Li San said, which was true enough. His father was chained to a stake as well. "Move closer to me, or we'll both freeze."

"I don't care," Hu said.

"Eh, I see." Li San was silent for a while. "Son," he asked finally, "were you guilty of stealing?"

"No!" said Hu. "I'm not a criminal, even if you are!"

"I know," said Li San. "I know you're not a criminal. There are always two sides to real stories. I'm going to tell you mine, whether you like it or not."

Hu said nothing. He hugged his knees tighter.

"You know I'm not from Beicheng."

Hu knew that. But he didn't know where his father was from or why he'd moved.

"My family lived down south, on an estate owned by a big landlord," Li San continued. The chain clinked as he talked. "We had to pay him a third of everything we grew. One year, many of the crops were ruined, like this year. The landlord came and said he wanted our whole harvest for taxes. If my mother had given it to him, we would have starved. So I sold our share before he could get it. He found out eventually. I was tried for theft and sent up here as punishment."

"You didn't actually steal anything?" Hu said.

"No, but the landlord thought I did."

"That's not fair!"

"Shh, son. Talking like that only brings more trouble."

But nothing seemed fair to Hu. Even if Li San had done something wrong the first time, that didn't mean he was guilty of stealing this time. Hu hadn't stolen anything on purpose either. He moved closer to his father.

"I'm sorry to get you into trouble again," he whispered. He told his father about his deal with Ren and their training together for the tournament.

Li San laughed at the bits about hiding in the toilet and Ren wearing Mei's trousers.

"It's not funny anymore," Hu said.

"May as well laugh," said Li San. "Some things are funny, even if the rest of life is as miserable as the underworld. Shame you can't just shoot your way out of trouble like Archer Yi. But don't you even think about it," he warned.

"Why can't we escape?" Hu said hopefully. His father was strong. He'd be able to get the stakes out of the ground if he tried, for sure.

"Perhaps we could," said Li San. "But I'm not leaving your mother. I've survived hard labor once. If we shut up and keep our heads down, maybe we can do it again."

"What will happen to our family?" Hu asked. "Will they be safe?"

"I don't know," Li San said sadly. "It's going to be hard for them."

Hu felt the icy fingers around his throat again. His father put one arm over Hu and pulled him close until they lay curled together. *Like noodles in a bowl,* Hu thought as he fell into an exhausted sleep.

During the day, Hu was often separated from Li San. There was nothing either of them could do about it. It was just that his father was much older and stronger, so he was given all the backbreaking work to do. The soldiers treated Hu as their personal slave, there to do all the dirty jobs. He lost count of how many privy pots he had emptied into a pit and scrubbed clean. At least none of the soldiers followed him too closely when he did that job. The stink kept them away.

"If ya even think of running off," one of the guards threatened, "I'll make ya wish ya'd never been born!"

As the winter set in, the privies froze over at night and it took twice as long to tip them out. One day, as Hu was chipping off the top layer of solid muck with a stone, Mei appeared.

"What are you doing here?" Hu said, alarmed. It was good to see his sister again, but what would happen if the soldiers saw her? He looked over his shoulder. The soldier who'd sent him out with the pot was complaining to another guard.

"Just keep your voice down and keep working," Mei said. "They can't see me here on the other side of this bush. I brought these."

Mei took half a dozen turnips out of her jacket.

Hu made himself smile at her before he went back to his work. "Thanks," he said. "Turnips are about as rare as mud here."

"Sorry," said Mei. "It's all we've got to eat."

"Us too. Is everything all right since . . . ?" Hu couldn't bring himself to say "since I was arrested." That was when he'd last seen Mei, Ma, and Ah-po.

Mei half shrugged her shoulders and fidgeted with her hair. "We're staying with the vegetable seller."

"And his six kids?" said Hu.

"We sleep on the floor. Tell our dad we're managing," she said. She dropped her voice. "Don't tell him this yet, not till afterward—I'm going to be married next month, at New Year."

Hu stopped digging at the pot and gaped at her. "Are you kidding?"

She turned pink and shook her head.

"Aren't you too young? Who are you getting married to?" Hu asked.

"I'm not that young. We need somewhere to live, Hu. Someone to look after us. People in Beicheng don't treat us like they used to. They're all hungry, and they think it's our fault."

Hu hadn't thought of that. It would be no fun being the family of a criminal. Especially a criminal who was supposed to have stolen other people's food.

"Who are you marrying?" Hu asked again.

"Ah-po helped arrange it. Ma's agreed too."

"Eh. So who is it?" Hu wondered what his sister might be hiding.

Mei took a deep breath. "You know that tall soldier who

used to come to the noodle stall?" Hu looked blank. "He got your bow back, remember?"

"Big Ears?" Hu exclaimed. "That oversized oaf who looks like a giant slobbering puppy? You can't marry him!"

"I can and I'm going to," Mei answered. "It's the best I can do. To keep us all safe while you're both up here. We'll be fine. He's not so bad."

Yes, he was. The thought of that soldier putting his great paws on his sister disgusted Hu. Surely Mei could do better. But then Hu realized that no one from Beicheng would want to marry a girl from a criminal family. Mei wouldn't have many men to choose from.

Hu wished the army had never come to Beicheng. He wished none of this had ever happened. He'd tried to make his life better and safer, and instead things had ended up far worse.

"Look, I brought something to show you," Mei said. She took something small from her sleeve. "He gave me this as a wedding present, along with some cloth. Tip that stuff out," she said, pointing to the privy, "and come and have a look."

Hu did as she suggested. It was a bronze ornament. "It's broken in half," Hu scoffed.

"Bronze doesn't break," said Mei. "It's meant to be that way."

"Then half of it must be lost," Hu said.

"Perhaps. I think it's beautiful."

It was beautiful. It was in the shape of an animal—a snarling tiger. Words were engraved across its back—the Chinese characters looked like dancing acrobats, each one poised and balanced.

"What does it say?" Hu asked.

"I don't know. He can't read either."

Hu knew she was referring to her future husband but was too embarrassed to say so.

"Where did he get it from?" Hu asked suspiciously.

"Not sure. He went away to Wuzhong for a while. Then he came back with this."

"You better hide it," said Hu. "It might be stolen."

"Don't think so," said Mei. "He's not perfect, but he's pretty honest. He said an official didn't want it. But I know where to keep it safe." She made a rude noise.

Hu snorted. He knew where she meant.

"Hey, you!" The soldier on guard at the watchtower yelled at Hu from his post. "Who are you talking to?"

"A relative," Hu called back.

"Tell 'em this isn't a family picnic. They can get out of here or I'll shoot." To prove his words, the guard put an arrow to his bow and lifted it to shoulder height.

"Go," Hu said to Mei.

So she went. Back to town and turnips, Ma and Ah-po. Gone to married life with a stranger. Like all the other good things in his life, Hu missed her so much.

He realized he hadn't even wished her good luck.

REN

"Don't know why you want to go there," said the cart driver for at least the third time. He was waiting for Ren to answer, but Ren didn't want to.

"They say there's going to be fighting," said the driver. "Most folks are trying to get out. I carried half the Magistrate's household out before. Thought I'd have to come back empty till I picked up you two."

In Wuzhong there had been no boat or horse willing to take Ren and Lien to Beicheng. The best Ren had been able to find was this donkey cart. They'd traveled very slowly and eaten awful food for over ten days. On the first day, the cart driver had wanted to take some stuff to a relative in a village off the road, and they had no choice but to go with him. In the end it was probably a good thing, Ren thought, because if Master Wang had sent someone after them, they would never have thought of looking out there.

The donkey cart bumped and swayed around another bend cut into the cliff.

"Big Brother," Lien shouted, "it's Beicheng!"

Beicheng looked different from the first time Ren had arrived at the town. Then, it had been hot and the sun had glinted off the battalion's weaponry. Now the yellow dust had turned to frozen mud. The donkey's hooves clopped and slipped as the animal made its way wearily up the steep road. The river below was still. It had a white icy sheen. The town looked small and gray. The Wall above it looked even smaller.

How could a dotted line of mud bricks keep out hordes of wild horsemen? Ren wondered. He had studied history, thanks to Master Wang. He knew that the barbarians had burned down the old capital once. What would they do to a little country town like Beicheng, if they really invaded? Seven months ago, he'd been disappointed when Second Deputy had said there'd be no fighting. Now he wished Second Deputy had been right and Beicheng was safe. Seven months ago, Ren and his sister had come in proudly, behind the Commander and his banners. This time Ren wasn't supposed to be here at all.

As they rattled and creaked up to Beicheng's gate, Ren thought over his plan. He had to find Hu first, then Hu could take Lien up to the town hall.

"Halt!" called the guards at the gate.

"Don't look up," Ren whispered to Lien. He didn't want the guards to recognize them, in case they reported back to the Commander.

"What've you got there?" the guards demanded to know.

"Empty cart and two passengers. Only kids," the cart driver answered.

"Go through," said the soldier. "Ought to search you properly, but we've got a lot to do and no reinforcements. Ye don't look like barbarians to me. Remember—no entry or exit after drumroll at dusk."

"Yes, sir." The driver flicked his reins. The donkey dipped its head and plodded through.

They were back. The cart driver headed up the main road

toward the marketplace and Hu's house. Ren kept thinking how good it would be to see him again. He wanted to tell Hu about everything he'd discovered, how he'd escaped and even brought his little sister back too. Hu would say something stupid and funny, but Ren knew he'd be interested.

As the donkey plodded through the market, Ren noticed there was nobody buying and selling. Instead, the townspeople were building a new stairway up to the town wall. The stairway was in the place where Hu's house had stood. Hu's house was gone.

Ren was worried. The faces of the townspeople looked thin and tight, as if they were already besieged by cold and creeping hunger.

And Hu was not there among them.

HU

Not much snow had fallen this dry, bleak winter, but cold and fear gripped everyone. Hu thought he would freeze as he worked. He worked until his arms and legs felt like they were made of sludge and grit, not skin and bones. The gap in the Wall had been leveled, but it was still only partly rebuilt. There were no signs of any barbarians.

"Might be waiting for the spring thaw," said some.

"Or waiting for the full moon, like wolves," said others.

The officers were uneasy and drove the men to work harder. Especially Hu and his father. Sometimes they even worked at night, when the moon gave enough light. But they weren't allowed to have fires to keep warm, in case the guards on watch down in Beicheng mistook the flames for a signal fire.

One day, toward evening, a soldier called Hu aside. "You!" he shouted. "Over here!"

Hu trudged after him to the soldiers' quarters inside the tower. He'd already done the privy pot that morning. What did they want now? He tripped over the doorway in his tiredness.

When he looked up, there was Ren.

Ren had the bow and the quiver of arrows over his shoulder. He was dressed in a long, padded coat edged in fur. He looked a bit older and a lot like a nobleman. Ren didn't smile in greeting. No one ever smiled at Hu these days.

Hu wondered what the Commander's son was doing there. Ren was supposed to be gone. Well, it was none of Hu's business now.

"That's the one," said Ren, nodding at the soldier. "I'll take him. He can empty the slops on the way."

He motioned to Hu to come after him. Hu followed him through the building site, carrying a basketful of rubbish. Ren led the way over the new Wall foundations into the forest on the other side, until they reached the clearing where they had practiced shooting in summer.

The grass was dead, and the leaves had long since fallen from the trees. The branches looked like black bones. *An army of skeletons,* thought Hu. He shivered. He wondered what Ren wanted.

"How about you dump that muck," said Ren. "It was the only excuse I could think of to come where people couldn't hear us."

Hu tipped the basket out as he was told.

"You don't look very good," Ren said to Hu, staring at the iron collar around his neck.

Hu didn't answer. He didn't feel very good either, but no way was he going to share his sorrows with Ren. It had been helping Ren that had gotten him into trouble, and Ren hadn't been there to help Hu in return when he needed it. Instead, when Hu had told the truth to the Magistrate, it had only made things worse for him and Li San. Hu preferred to keep his distance from the Commander's son. He didn't trust Ren.

"Can I go back to camp then, *sir*?" Hu said.

"Aren't you glad I've rescued you?" said Ren.

Hu was not glad. He had always been the sort of person that hoped for the best, but he'd been wrong. He'd thought the worst had already happened to him, but perhaps it hadn't. At least till now he'd had the comfort of his father's presence every night, but now Ren might be here to take him away.

"I don't want to be rescued by you," he said bitterly.

"Don't you realize how much trouble it's been for me?" Ren said. "First I had to get back to Beicheng. Then you weren't there, so I had to find your family. They're looking after my sister for me. They said you were up here. But they didn't tell me about that." Ren pointed at the collar.

Hu clenched his jaw. He was bristling inside with feelings as sharp as a quiverful of arrows.

"I made up that I had orders to move you," Ren went on. "I showed the guard in the garrison this." Ren took out a scroll from inside his coat. He grinned. "Just as well the dummy can't read."

Ren looked pleased with himself—smug as a fed fox.

"I didn't ask you to come," Hu said. His words came out hard as iron. "I don't want to see you again. Go away and leave me alone."

"But you're my only friend." Ren frowned. "I'm already in huge trouble with my father. I'm not supposed to be here. He sent me away! I haven't got anyone else," he pleaded. "Why stay here? You can leave and help me."

"You want *me* to get *you* out of trouble?" Hu said. Sometimes Ren was unreal. He expected the whole world to fit in with his ideas. He was so wrapped up in himself, he couldn't see how things were for others. "Do you even know what trouble means? Who's going to listen to *me*?"

Hu's voice was rising.

"When *you* get into trouble, you miss out on a banquet

or you get homework. Or maybe you get sent away to some-where safe. You poor boy! Look at me!" Hu shouted. "I'm a criminal for stealing grain I never touched. I got an iron collar and a tattoo. My sister's got to marry one of your 'dummy' soldiers to survive. My dad and me, we've got to work out here for three years, if we last that long. If the work doesn't kill us, then we could still starve. Or the barbarians will come and swat us like flies. So get lost!"

Ren looked shaken.

Good, thought Hu. He wanted to make Ren suffer. It served him right for being so rich and selfish. If there had ever been a real friendship between them, it was over, he thought. Hu was not Ren's equal and never would be. No matter how hard he worked or how well he could shoot.

"I'm returning to duty, *sir*," Hu said. He bowed stiffly to Ren and turned back to the camp.

"No—wait!" called Ren. "Please!"

Hu ignored him. It was getting dark. A low rumble of drums growled around the Beicheng valley. The town gates were closing. Li San would be wondering where Hu was. His dad might get into trouble with the guards if he didn't get back soon.

"Stop!" Ren called. "Don't go back there!"

Hu dragged his aching feet wearily toward the garrison.

Then something hit him in the calf, so sharp and sudden it knocked him over.

REN

"What's the matter?" said Ren. "Are you all right?"

Hu groaned and propped himself up on his hands and knees. "Right as rain," he said, his head hanging down.

"Come on, then. We've got to get out of here, back to Beicheng. Did you see where the arrow went?"

"Arrow?" said Hu.

"Yes, the one I just shot past here. So you'd stop being stupid. Forget it! Let's get moving."

It was getting harder to see.

Hu pressed his lips together. They went white. He grabbed a low-hanging tree branch to pull himself up, and cracked a crooked smile. Or maybe it wasn't a smile at all.

"I'm right, all right," Hu said, through clenched teeth. "As right as rain when there's a hole in the roof." Then his leg twisted out from underneath him and he toppled sideways.

Ren looked at him with surprise and sudden fear. There was often more to Hu than he expected. Hu was not crying on the ground like a baby. But he was definitely not all right. There was something about his leg that was strange. The shape was crooked. Ren looked more closely.

Hu's foot skewed at a funny angle. Halfway down Hu's left shin, the end of the arrow stuck out of his trousers.

Ren felt a wave of nausea. He'd shot the arrow to get

Hu's attention. To stop him walking away and make him listen. It was meant to go wide. But the light was bad.

"Stupid!" he yelled. He yelled it at Hu, but it could have been at himself. "Why didn't you listen?"

Hu's words were ringing in his ears. Master Wang had fixed the blame on Hu and Li San for the missing grain supplies, and now they were convicts. It wasn't fair. Ren realized he could do nothing to help them, because the Commander would never believe him.

Hu didn't answer. Ren didn't know much about injuries, but it was obvious he couldn't walk.

Hu's face was white as a ghost's in the faint light.

Fear rose in Ren's throat, choking him. He knew Hu could die if he left him lying there in the dark and the cold. It had been foolhardy to think he could rescue Hu, but even if he couldn't get Hu out of hard labor, he could get him out of the forest.

Ren stood up.

"This is your fault. Don't you leave me," Hu croaked as he lay on the ground. His eyes were deep black and fixed on Ren.

"I'm going to get help," Ren said. He wondered if he could hold down the nausea rising inside him.

"You better, you sly, selfish bastard," Hu spat out.

Ren didn't look back. Hu's accusations shot into him and made him hurry faster. As he scrambled through the shadows toward the Great Wall, he thought he could feel Hu's eyes watching, burning into his back. There wasn't time to argue with Hu now. Ren would prove his promise by getting help as fast as he could.

Ren stumbled over a rock and nearly fell. In the dark the forest was a host of vague, looming shadows. Ren slowed up so as not to get lost. He concentrated on remembering the way back to the Wall. In the distance he thought he could see the garrison tower outlined against the night sky. Past the ridge in front, he remembered, he had to cross a long gully full of thick bushes. It was barely a bowshot to the break in the Wall.

Ren thought he heard a wolf howl, a long way off. He remembered what Hu had said about seeing a tiger near here. He hoped tigers didn't prowl in the dark. Wolves were bad enough. At least he had the bow, but Hu had no protection at all.

Twigs and branches flicked at him as he went down into the gully. Ren slowed even more and listened to the night. He wished he had a horse. Traveling on horseback was a lot safer and faster.

Then he heard a horse whinny, soft and snorting. Ren thought it must be his own wishful thinking. No—there was a gentle clop of hooves. The sound was indistinct but coming closer. Soldiers had probably come looking for Hu. Ren nearly called out, but had second thoughts and stopped himself. He would see which officer it was first. He crouched behind a bush.

The sound of hooves was very quiet. Just when Ren thought he must have been imagining things, the shadowy outline of a horse went past. Then a second one. And a third one. And a whole lot more. Ren lost count of how many there were. It was hard to tell in the dark. It seemed like a muffled procession of hundreds of horses, with silent riders. Ren began to wonder if they were ghosts. His heart beat harder. He told himself he was being stupid and stayed completely still.

Finally the hooves and the blurred shapes stopped. There

was a thud as the rider nearest to Ren dismounted. And the metallic clunk of a sword in its sheath.

No one shouted any orders. No one lit a torch.

Finally, up the line, one of the riders spoke softly, and the message came down toward Ren.

The words sounded strange in the night air. Distorted. Like a stream burbling over pebbles. The rider next to Ren's bush grunted and replied, still with the same burbling sound.

It was then Ren realized why the riders sounded so strange. They weren't speaking Chinese. They were bar- barians.

HU

When Ren had left, the darkness had closed around Hu like a coffin.

He had tried to move, to get up and follow Ren. But even shifting his weight on the ground bumped the arrow shaft and darts of pain shot up his leg. If he lay on his side, completely still, it didn't hurt so much.

The cold from the ground was an iron vice that held him. Hu's leg became a dull, gray ache that took over his brain. He was sure Ren would not come back. He didn't want to stay out here alone, but he couldn't think what to do.

Somewhere a long way off, a wolf howled.

The moon rose above the black bushes, but clouds swirled across it and it didn't give much light. It was nearly full. The last full moon for the year of the Tiger. Funny that the new moon after this one would be New Year. There should be lots of people and food and performances. His mother singing, his father acting . . . But that would never happen again.

The memories faded into dark and pain. The cold was like stone in his bones.

Somewhere not far off, a wild goose called.

Hu wished he had wings.

A wild goose calling? At night? Ah-po used to tell a story about a bird that took people to Heaven. Had it come for him?

The bird called again.

"Here," said Hu. His voice came out as a whisper. His funny old Ah-po was right about some things.

Heaven would be better than lying here. *Anything* would be better than lying here. He couldn't stand it much longer. He called again. "I'm here."

"Then shut up!" hissed a voice. It wasn't a bird at all. "Keep dead quiet, or we've had it."

A figure dived beside Hu, under the bush. It knocked Hu's leg, and a jab of fire passed through him. Hu cried out. A hand clamped over his mouth.

"Shut up, I tell you!"

It sounded like Ren. What was Ren doing here? Hu's brain felt frozen and time was going around in circles inside his head.

Ren's voice whispered in Hu's ear, "The barbarian army is camped between us and the Wall. Right near the breach. I can't reach the garrison. I need to know: is there any other way of getting across the Wall?"

Hu groaned. "No." He and his father and the other workers had fixed up the rest of the Wall near Beicheng. They had pounded and pounded and pounded the earth, the way his wound was pounding now.

"We can't stay here," Ren hissed at him insistently. "By dawn this place will be swarming."

Hu had trouble focusing on what Ren was saying. But somehow Ren's voice was pulling him out of his black box, back to the land of the living.

"What?" said Hu.

"I said we can't stay here — are you sure there's no other way to Beicheng?"

"The Wall goes straight down to the river," Hu answered with an effort.

"Between us and Beicheng all the way?" Ren asked.

"Yeah."

"What does it do at the river?" Ren asked.

"Stops. At the top of the cliff." What a dumb question. Hu barely had the energy for talking. All he could think about was his leg.

"Is there a way down the cliff?"

He forced himself to concentrate. "Yes. There's a path. Then you have to swim. Except you can't. The river bends — over rocks."

"How far is it?" Ren asked.

"Don't know. Fifteen miles or something, all the way back." Fifteen miles or a thousand, it didn't matter. There was no way Hu could make it there. His muscles were freezing up. He could hardly get words out of his mouth.

Ren said nothing. Hu waited for him to leave like he had before. He might as well. Even if, by some miracle and with Ren's help, Hu hobbled all the way to the river, there was no way either of them could struggle through the rapids.

"Do you have anything to eat? Like a bun?" Ren asked him.

How could Ren be thinking of food? Of course he had no bun, and if he did, what good would it do either of them? The cold felt like fire now, burning into his bones. Burning upward from the metal in his leg.

"No food at all? Because I've got an idea."

"Here," Hu reached inside the fold of his jacket and pulled out his last turnip. He chucked it at Ren.

"Ow!" Ren rubbed his face. "Perfect!" he said.

Ren was really strange, Hu thought. What was so wonderful about a turnip? "You wouldn't say that if you'd had nothing else to eat for months," Hu told him.

"Well, you would if you were a horse," Ren said. "I'll be back soon. I hope." Ren put his bow down beside Hu, then took off his coat and tossed it over him. "Mind these."

Then he sneaked off purposefully, running low like a wolf.

Ren made no sense. Nothing made any sense. But it was warm under Ren's coat. Hu dreamed, of horses and wolves and wild geese in the night. It began to snow.

"Goose feathers falling," he heard Ah-po say.

REN

At the edge of the gully, Ren slowed to a crawl.

Before him, in the darkness, were the barbarian horsemen. He couldn't hear them, and he couldn't see them, but unless they were all ghosts or he was mad, they were there.

Ren didn't know exactly how many of them had already arrived. When he'd stumbled across them the first time, it had taken forever for them to file past. Ren vaguely remembered an old story about an army that was so vast it stretched from one horizon to another. The gully wasn't big enough to hide that many horsemen. It couldn't hold enough for an invasion, which probably meant this was a raiding party. They might have come just to steal, burn, and run. Or they might be just the forward troops, and more were coming. . . .

Either way, right in front of him were more than enough horsemen to chase down one boy in the forest.

But they weren't after him, not yet, at least. They had some bigger plan. And there were enough of them to take on the Tiger Battalion, easily. With the gap in the Wall not yet rebuilt, the soldiers in the garrison would not be able to hold them off. The invaders would be at the walls of Beicheng before anybody could do anything. Ren had no way of knowing when the barbarians would strike. But he was sure it would happen before dawn, when they would be spotted from the watchtower on the Wall.

Ren had to get back to Beicheng, and fast. Which was why he was back there, lurking at the edge of the enemy camp.

He held his breath to listen. The barbarian troops were very good at hiding. But every now and then, perhaps because he knew what to listen for, Ren could hear horse noises—little clinks and snorts. He got down on his stomach and slithered under the bushes toward them.

It was snowing. Ren felt the cold flakes on the back of his neck, melting down inside his collar. He wished he could have worn his fur-lined coat, but it was so thick it would have gotten in the way.

Ren clamped his jaws together to stop his teeth from chattering. He heard a few foreign words, very soft, off to his right. His heartbeat pulsed through his whole body. He headed left.

And there, right in front of him, nearly stepping on his head, was a horse. Its hooves were tied up in rags, to muffle the sound of its movements. Ren knew he mustn't frighten it. He reached a shaking hand inside his top and took out Hu's turnip. The turnip was warm from being carried against his body; it had a faint, sweet smell of grassy fields.

Very slowly, Ren pulled his legs up under him, and sat in a squat. He shuffled closer to the horse. He held out his empty hand to the animal and let it sniff. The horse wasn't interested in the empty hand. It wanted the turnip, but it couldn't reach. Its reins were tied around a branch.

Ren bit off a piece of turnip and offered it to the horse, stroking its warm nose. Then he stood up carefully. His knees clicked. The horse shied away slightly.

Ren didn't dare talk to it. He broke off another bit of turnip and fed it to the animal, and then he untied the reins. He noticed the horse was still saddled. He guessed that meant the barbarians didn't intend to stay in one place for long.

Ren held the last piece of vegetable underneath the horse's nose. When he felt its warm breath over his hand, he withdrew the turnip and took a step back. The horse followed. Ren backed up the slope, tugging gently on the reins. The horse came with him, snorting after the turnip. If he could just get the horse over the rise without anyone noticing, he could ride down the other side. He'd get back to Hu and his bow in no time. Then they'd ride for Beicheng like all the ghouls of the underworld were after them.

He was nearly there. He tried to pick up speed.

Three-quarters of the way up the slope, he tripped over a log and fell to the ground with a thump. The horse whinnied. Ren heard voices, then twigs crunching underfoot. Any second now they would be coming up here after him. He had to distract them, fast.

What will make them turn back? he thought in a panic.

What? What? If he howled like a wolf that would upset all the horses—his horse too. It was hard enough to get a strange horse to trust you without the animal thinking you were about to eat it.

Ren felt around on the ground and picked up a couple of small rocks. He threw them high, in the direction of the barbarians' camp. A horse whinnied, down in the gully. Bull's-eye, as Hu would say. In the dark, nobody would know what had disturbed the horse, but it would make them all jittery, for sure. The footsteps went away from him, back to the camp, and Ren led the stolen horse over the top of the rise.

HU

The next thing Hu knew, something was breathing clouds of steam all over his face. Some monstrous animal stood right over him, snuffing and snorting, blacking out the moon.

He tried to scream, but it came out as a croak. "Help!"

"I'm back," said Ren's voice from somewhere behind the creature. "We can go. Get on the horse."

So that was what it was—a horse. Hu had never ridden one before. He would rather be on it than under it, like he was now. But he had no idea how to mount. Or even how to stand up.

"Hurry up. We have to get back to Beicheng to warn my father." Ren took back his coat. The icy air made Hu shiver. He struggled to sit up.

"How do I get on that thing?" he asked.

"We haven't got a mounting block, and I can't lift you," Ren said impatiently. "You'll need to stand on a stump or a rock and throw your leg over."

And turtles can fly, thought Hu. It was impossible. "I can't climb onto a rock," he said.

"Barbarian horses aren't that tall," Ren said. "It's just a pony. You're an acrobat. Can't you jump or something?"

Hu thought with a pang of Li San, who could lift anyone. His father would be lying in the dark, in his hut beside the gap in the Wall, worrying about Hu. Li San wouldn't realize his own life was in danger. He didn't know there was only a part-built wall between him and a barbarian army.

"We've got to warn the garrison," Hu said to Ren. "Or all the workers will be killed."

"We can't," Ren said. "I've already told you, the barbarians are between us and the watchtower. That's why I've got this horse—to go around the long way. Hurry up—they might come after us."

"Won't the soldiers notice them?"

"Not at night, with the moon half under clouds, and snow to deaden the noise. I didn't know they were there until I almost ran into them. The garrison won't know anything until it's attacked."

Until it's attacked . . . That would be too late for Li San. Unless . . .

"Help me stand up," Hu said.

Ren put one of Hu's arms around his neck and took most of his weight.

"One, two, three . . ." Ren heaved Hu to his feet.

Hu looked at the waiting pony. The saddle was about shoulder height. Not too high, but high enough when his leg felt like it was full of boiling, spitting oil.

Hu put one hand on each rim of the saddle, front and back. Then he pushed down through his arms, like an acrobat vaulting. He pointed the toes of his one good foot, and swung it up and over, neat as a pair of scissors.

He nearly toppled off the other side. Ren grabbed him by the arm to steady him. He'd done it—he was on the pony. It hurt, but his success helped clear his head.

"Watch it!" Ren said. "You made me tip the quiver." Ren felt around on the ground in the dark. "I can only find three arrows."

"You got your bow?" Hu said.

"Yes, but it won't be much use if they come after us. Can't see to shoot at night." Ren mounted the pony behind Hu and turned it toward the river.

But Hu had an idea. "Turn around and go back up the ridge. Remember Archer Yi? Shot the sun?"

"Are you crazy? Right now it's pitch black," Ren said. "We could do with some sun."

"There's the watchtower," Hu said. "If you shoot at that, they'll light the fire. The garrison'll think it's under attack. We've just got to warn them, and they'll warn Beicheng."

"But we can't go back that way," Ren said. "How would we get past the barbarians?"

"We can't cross the gully—but an arrow can. That will be enough to let the garrison know someone is out here." Ren might not care about Hu's father, thought Hu, but he did.

Ren took a deep breath.

Then he turned the horse back. Toward the watchtower, the Wall, and the enemy army.

At the top of the ridge, above the gully, they stopped. A bowshot away, the watchtower made a solid black silhouette against the cloud-streaked sky.

Ren took the bow off his back. "You shoot," he whispered to Hu. "You're better than me."

It was the first time Ren had ever said that, and Hu could tell it was hard for him to admit it. But tonight he was wrong. Hu had used his last energy to haul himself up onto the horse and was barely holding himself on. He didn't have the strength to draw a bow.

"I can't," said Hu, "not now, but you can."

"Are you sure?" whispered Ren.

Hu nodded. He began to sing, very, very softly. *"Legendary archer Yi fits an arrow to his bow and draws . . ."*

Ren dismounted. He nocked an arrow on the string. Then he drew the string back and held it taut against his cheek. He released. Hu could hear the arrow in a quick rush of air through the night. Then there was silence.

Nothing happened. There was no sound from either the barbarian camp or the Wall.

"Aren't they going to light the fire or beat the drum or something?" Ren muttered.

"Maybe you missed," Hu said. "You've got three arrows. Try again. *The archer takes aim. He is nearly blinded—he pauses.*"

A wolf howled. Unpleasantly close. The horse started. Ren grabbed the reins to stop it from bolting off, and made reassuring noises.

"Ren," Hu whispered. "What if that's not a real wolf?"

"Just don't talk about ghosts at a time like this," Ren hissed.

"I mean—you weren't a real wild goose. Perhaps it's a signal?"

Ren stood firm and shot the second arrow into the night. The bowstring thrummed.

Still there was no response from the tower. But from the gully slope there came a sound like snow crunching underfoot.

"Enemy scouts," Ren whispered.

"Last chance," Hu whispered back. Maybe the enemy would kill them. But unless they could raise the alarm, the barbarians would kill everyone. There would be no home to return to, no life as they used to know it.

"One unswerving arrow will bring down the sun. One arrow will carry his fame to the heavens . . ."

Ren fitted the last arrow, drew, and released. The arrow flew into the night, over the heads of the enemy, straight to the watchtower. Or so Hu hoped.

Immediately Ren slung the bow over his shoulder. He jumped onto the horse behind Hu and kicked it into action. The pony clattered off down toward the river, just as a group of shadowy figures emerged from the bushes onto the snow.

REN

"Have they seen us?" Hu asked, as the pony cantered through the clearing.

An arrow whistled overhead.

"Hold on!" Ren yelled. He made the horse turn sharply to the left, out of the moonlight and into the trees. Another arrow thwacked into a nearby tree trunk.

Ren turned the horse again, right this time.

Hu was flopping around like a sack of grain, making it harder to control the horse.

"Duck!" Ren cried out, as the pony barged under a low-hanging branch. Twigs scraped across their faces. Dark branches swiped them.

More arrows whooshed into the snow—behind them. That was good. The horse was pulling ahead of the barbarians, who were only on foot.

Ren put an arm around Hu. He was worried Hu would pass out, and he was a useless rider, though Ren had to admire the way he'd gotten himself onto the horse. He was small, but tough, like the pony.

Ren wondered what the barbarians might do next. Maybe go back to their camp to get horses and more men. He looked over his shoulder—there was nothing to be seen but shadows.

Ren let the pony slow down and pick its way through the dark forest. Horses were smart. It was wise to let this one find its own route, as long as he kept it parallel to the Wall, which appeared occasionally as a straight shadow in the moonlight.

"We've lost them. For now anyway," he said to Hu.

"Did your last arrow reach the tower?" Hu asked.

"I don't know," said Ren. There hadn't been time to watch or listen for a response. They'd had to run.

"It probably won't make any difference," Ren said despairingly. "There aren't enough troops to protect Beicheng for long anyway. My father asked the Emperor for the other half of the tiger tally ages ago, but in Beicheng they said the reinforcements never came."

"What did you say?" Hu asked. "He asked for what?"

"Fresh orders and reinforcements. That means extra soldiers."

"And the tiger? What's that?"

Ren was uneasy. Maybe that was a military secret and he wasn't supposed to tell Hu. But then, he and Hu and the whole Tiger Battalion might all be dead before long, so it wouldn't matter.

"Tally. It's this little tiger object made out of bronze. The Emperor gives one half to the Commander, with his orders, and keeps the other half. If the orders change, like, say, the Commander is told to attack or withdraw, then the Emperor sends the second half out."

"It's made out of bronze?" Hu said. "With character writing on it?"

"Yes. So? What does it matter now?"

"I think my sister has it."

"Your sister?" Ren was astounded. "She has the Emperor's tally?"

Then he was furious. So Hu's family really were thieves. Of the worst sort. Traitors! And he had entrusted his little sister to them in Beicheng.

He pulled the horse up suddenly and gave Hu a shove. "You can lie here in the dark to die. You thief! It will serve you right when you're murdered by the barbarians."

Hu lurched forward and clutched the horse's mane.

"She didn't steal it," he said. "A man gave it to her—it was an engagement present. The big, bumbling soldier who used to guard the town hall—Big Ears."

Ren guessed immediately which soldier Hu was talking about—the same soldier who had accompanied Master Wang, himself, and Lien to Wuzhong. The discovery of the barbarian army had pushed Master Wang and the grain right out of Ren's mind. But perhaps Master Wang had interfered with the Emperor's reply to the Commander, and Mei's "present" was actually the missing tally.

"Right," Ren said. "We've got to get it. As fast as we can." He held on to Hu and spurred the horse forward again.

They followed the line of the Wall southward toward the river. After a while, Hu went very quiet. Ren could feel his friend's weight against his own chest. Every now and then a big shiver seemed to pass through Hu's body, and he would slip a bit on the horse. One of Ren's arms was going numb with Hu leaning on it. Ren was worried that Hu might fall off. Or even die . . . He was not sure what it took to kill someone. An arrow in the leg didn't sound as deadly as one in the heart, but Hu didn't seem too good.

Ren wondered what would happen if Hu died in his

arms. Would he know when Hu was dead? Might Hu's ghost haunt him forever, to punish Ren for shooting him?

Hu needed help. Ren needed help. But there were no friends to be found in the forest, only enemies.

The night was deathly quiet. The moon shone through the clouds occasionally. Ren remembered an eerie song about the moon goddess Hu's mother had sung at the performance.

Ren had never paid attention when he went to the temple with his family—the ceremonies for ancestors were always so boring. So he couldn't remember which god was which, and he didn't know how to pray. He remembered all the levels of Heaven he'd seen painted on temple walls. Would the prayer of a mere boy like him even make it to the King of Heaven? Did the Immortals do stuff for you, or did you have to do things for them first?

The pony jolted down a steep slope. Hu moaned and slumped farther forward. Ren was desperate. He would try praying to someone who knew what it was like to be human.

"Legendary Archer Yi," he began, in his head so Hu wouldn't hear. "Or whoever is listening . . . Most Honorable Immortal, I'm sorry I don't know the proper prayers. It's my fault, but could you please help? Get us home safe. Please help Hu stay alive, and help him stay on this horse for long enough to get the other half of the tiger and get to safety. If you do I'll . . ." Ren tried to think of something appropriate to offer, something an Immortal might approve of. "If you get us out of this, I promise to copy out that chapter from the *Book of Rites* Master Wang wanted me to learn, in my best handwriting. I'll really try, if you will too. Please."

Ren stopped. He couldn't think of anything more to say. He tried to put his hands together in the polite manner for thanking someone, but Hu was leaning to one side.

Nothing much appeared to change. The pony kept plodding on steadily through the dark. The Wall loomed to their left—a high black shadow against the stars.

Hu was shaking with shivers now. Even on horseback, with the sweaty steam of the horse coming up around them, Ren could feel the cold. Hanging below the pony's warm flank, his toes were frozen. He tried not to think about Hu's torn leg dangling beside his and the arrow sticking out of it.

"Hu? Hu! Don't fall asleep or you might fall off." He had to keep Hu talking. If he was talking, he couldn't be dead.

Hu grunted.

Please stay alive, Ren thought.

HU

The darkness was closing in on Hu again. Every bump and jolt of the horse sent shudders of pain through him. He forgot where he was going and why. He just had to hold on. That was all he thought about.

"How much farther?" Ren asked.

That was the question running through Hu's head too, but his lips felt like they were iced together. "Don't know," he managed to get out.

"Do you remember what was written on the tiger?"

"Don't know," Hu answered.

"Don't go to sleep on me," said Ren urgently. "What did the characters say?"

The characters began to dance around in Hu's brain, teasing him.

"Can't read."

"Death and demons," Ren said.

Yes, thought Hu. It wouldn't be long before they both became ghosts.

The pony stopped. In front of them was a long drop. The river gleamed faintly below, like a gray pit. Hu could feel himself starting to topple forward. He was falling slowly as a goose feather. . . .

Ren yanked him back. "Now where?" he demanded.

Where? The path. "That way. Away from the Wall."

The pony wandered slowly along the cliff top. When Hu looked over the cliff's edge, dizziness came over him again.

"This it?" said Ren. The horse had found the steep track by itself. The animal's shoulders seemed to drop out from underneath Hu as it headed down. He gripped the saddle harder. The pony's cloth-wrapped hooves slithered on the icy ground.

"I'd better get off," Ren said.

Hu felt the freezing air in the gap where Ren had been sitting. Every time the horse took a step, it felt like the bottom of the world was falling out.

Ren made soothing noises to the pony. "That's it. That's the way, girl."

Finally, they stopped. The river glimmered at their feet.

"I can't swim it," said Hu. He was already frozen. In the water he'd seize up and sink like a stone.

Ren bent down at the water's edge. He picked up a pebble and threw it as far as he could, into the middle of the river.

Clink, clink, clink.

"Nobody can swim now," Ren said. He was smiling. "It's frozen solid, you dummy. All we've got to do is walk around the corner just over there, then we're back on the other side of the Wall. Beicheng, here we come!"

He clicked his tongue cheerfully at the pony and led it out onto the ice.

Then there was a sudden rush of air. *Thwack!*

Ren fell forward on the ice. Sticking out of the back of his coat was the shaft of an arrow.

"Ren!" Hu cried. He couldn't get off the horse. He was stuck. And Ren was dead.

But Ren stood up, shakily. His face was ghostly and

his eyes were wide. Then he scrambled onto the horse and kicked its flanks. The pony charged forward.

"They must have followed us," Ren shouted in Hu's ear. "And now they can see well enough to shoot."

Hu realized he and Ren were black figures on the white ice. A clear target.

But they were moving fast. The pony skidded and skittered across the white expanse.

Thwack! Hu felt the impact as another arrow hit Ren. He waited for Ren to topple from the horse, but he just held on tighter. They were level with where the wall stopped at the river.

A branch stuck out of the frozen rapids. One of the pony's hooves caught it in mid-stride. The horse was off-balance. The boys tipped to one side. *Crunch.* Hu hit the ice hard. Stars exploded in front of his eyes. He slid across the river's surface and crashed into Ren.

Ren lay still.

The pony rolled to its knees and shook its mane. Then it stood up. It didn't seem to be hurt.

Hu's body was racked with pain and cold. But there was nothing new in that.

Was Ren all right? The arrow shafts still poked out of his coat. Hu shook his shoulder. "Ren!"

"Agh," Ren groaned. "I'm winded." Hu heard him struggling to get his breath back. "Good thing . . ." he wheezed, "I've still got your father's old armor on. Ouch. Ice is hard."

If Ren could complain, he wasn't badly injured, Hu thought. He was relieved. Enough bad things had happened in one night, and he didn't want any more. He just wanted to get home.

"They've stopped shooting at us," Ren said. "Maybe they

think we're dead. Lie still a few more minutes, in case they're still watching."

They lay still and waited. Hu looked toward the shore. He couldn't see anything.

Hu's teeth began to chatter, and his arms and legs shook. No one came down onto the ice.

"Think we'd better g-go now," said Ren. His teeth were chattering too. "Or we *will* be d-dead."

Hu couldn't walk—he had to get back on the horse.

"Ren," he said, "c-c-can you kneel? My arms are sh-shaking. Can't l-lift myself. If I s-s-sit on your shoulders 'n you st-stand up, you can tip me onto the h-horse."

Ren hesitated. Then he knelt down in front of Hu. For one weird second Hu saw himself kneeling before the Magistrate. *"Sentenced to three years' hard labor,"* he heard a voice say in his head. Then Hu crawled and clawed his way onto Ren's shoulders. The arrows stayed stuck fast in the leather armor on Ren's back.

"Don't p-pull my hair," Ren said. He hoisted Hu onto the pony, and stood on the branch to pull himself up. "Let's get out of here."

The two boys rode around the corner. And there was Beicheng.

REN

The town was a raised black hump. No sound and no movement came from it. No sound or movement came from the river valley behind the boys either. *Thank the gods, or thank whoever,* thought Ren. It was amazing they had made it this far.

"First thing is to get the tiger tally," Ren said to Hu. "Once we're in."

He'd already planned how they would get inside. They were traveling around the back of the town wall toward the outside toilet.

"I'll climb up from on top of the toilet. Then, when I'm in, I'll get the guards to open up the gates for you and the horse. I'll be as quick as I can. You keep my coat while you're waiting."

"Can't," said Hu. "L-ladder's gone."

"Great," said Ren. The gates were locked too. After all it had taken to get there, now they were stuck outside the town wall.

"T-talk your way in," said Hu.

That was what Hu would do, Ren supposed, but Hu wasn't in a state to tell jokes. And Ren couldn't think of any. He didn't think the guards would be in the mood for them either.

Ren didn't want to alert the guards to who he was. He didn't know if they would believe him anyway, because he was supposed to be in the capital. But there was nothing for it. He had to get the tiger tally, and he had to warn the Commander, or they'd all be dead. Ren urged the pony on.

"Stop!" said Hu. His voice sounded pinched, as if he was having trouble opening his lips. "T-t-tiger!"

"Where?" said Ren in alarm.

"Toilet," Hu said.

"What?"

"My sister. D-don't have our own home. H-hid it."

Hu was not making sense.

"L-look," Hu said. He was pointing to the toilet. Hu was right about the ladder—the whole roof had been taken off, so it didn't provide a platform for climbing up. The toilet was a black pit open to the sky, with who knows what disgusting mess in it, but definitely no place for a tiger.

"The t-tally," said Hu.

All of a sudden Ren figured him out. "Do you mean your sister put the Emperor's tally in a *toilet*?"

"Mm," Hu grunted.

It made sense, in the funny way Hu's family had of looking at things. Nobody stayed in a toilet like that longer than they could help. Nobody looked for anything valuable in one. Ren sighed. Hu could not get on or off the horse, so Ren would have to go in there again himself, even though he'd sworn not to.

It took several minutes of unpleasant feeling around the walls, but finally Ren found the tally, tucked above a cross beam, wrapped in a rag. He passed the dirty bundle to Hu.

The pony plodded slowly up the snowy road to Beicheng's gates. It was tired. Who knew how far the animal had already traveled before Ren stole it? He patted its neck.

"There's a nice, warm stable and food waiting for you," he told the horse.

"Thanks," Hu mumbled.

"I wasn't talking to you," Ren said. He worried that Hu was slipping away. He urged the pony forward, until the town gates were towering over their heads, shut and barred against all comers.

Ren banged on one of the huge doors with his fist.

"*Wei, wei,* you on duty! Let me in," he called out.

A torch appeared on the sentry tower above them.

"The town's under curfew. No entry till dawn. Come back tomorrow," a voice shouted down.

By tomorrow there would be hundreds of horsemen surrounding the town, and he and Hu would be dead. Ren sat up in the saddle, trying to look as tall as possible. The guards probably couldn't see him well in the dark, which was a good thing.

"Open up in the name of the Emperor!" he yelled.

"We don't open up for nobody. Who do ya think ya are? Get lost or we'll shoot."

"I'm . . ." Ren paused. He didn't know whose voice it was behind the gate. What could he say to impress them, without giving himself away? "A nobleman!" he shouted up to the gate.

"You know the password?"

Ren tried to think. Who set the passwords? What excuse could he give for not knowing?

"Hurry up! Or shove off before we shoot," the sentry threatened. "Commander's orders."

Ren's mind was galloping. Commander's orders—yes, his father set the passwords. He'd seen him giving them to Second Deputy. But Ren hadn't been around for a month. He had no idea what tonight's password might be.

"If yer drunk, ya can stay out till the cold sobers ya up,"

came the guard's voice. "I have an arrow pointed straight at ya. A nobleman . . ."

Ren was angry. And scared too.

"C-come on," said Hu. "What's the rest? 'A nobleman . . .' what?"

So that was the start of the password! The guards were giving him a chance. They thought he knew all of it. But he didn't.

Confounded Confucius! Yes he did!

"A nobleman without integrity is like a chariot without an axle," Ren shouted.

No response.

Then inside the bolts squealed and clanged. One after another. Slowly, one of the gates grated along the ground and began to swing open.

Ren gripped Hu. Before the guards could ask questions, he spurred the horse forward and charged into the town.

HU

Ren and Hu staggered together into the courtyard of the town hall.

Torches were burning outside the Commander's quarters, and people were scurrying everywhere. A servant was saddling a horse as fast as he could. He was having trouble getting the straps in place. The Commander was pacing back and forth, wearing all his armor, even the winged shoulder pieces and his helmet. The torchlight threw huge, twisted shadows behind him. Hu thought he looked like the demon king of the underworld.

Commander Zheng was not at all pleased to see the boys. "Who are you to come in here? Clear out," he ordered.

Hu looked at Ren. In the torchlight he could see that the Commander's son had a swollen bump over one eye and a scrape down his cheek. His own father didn't recognize him.

"It's me, sir. Zheng Ren."

The Commander stood still and looked even less pleased. "Ren? What are you doing here? No, don't tell me now. Get to your room."

Hu could feel Ren shaking. Or maybe that was him. He just hoped Ren kept holding him up. He wished someone would come and take him off his feet, and take him somewhere safe. Pain smoldered inside him, eating his strength.

"Who's that boy?" Commander Zheng demanded. "Get him out of here."

Hu was too dizzy to speak. The torchlight and shadows were making his vision dance. He had trouble concentrating on the voices around him.

"He's . . ." Ren began.

What was Hu exactly? He wasn't sure himself. He was suddenly very aware of the iron ring around his neck. He wasn't an acrobat now. A criminal. Someone Ren used when it suited him and dumped when it didn't. Someone half-alive. Someone who wanted to be anywhere but here.

"He's my friend, Li Hu," Ren said.

Hu wasn't sure if he had heard right.

One of Commander Zheng's eyebrows shot up. "This is no place for either of you. If we survive this, I'll deal with you then. This town could be under attack within hours.

"Is my horse ready?" he shouted to the servant. He stepped on the mounting stool the servant put down for him, and swung his leg over the horse.

So they knew. One of Ren's arrows must have found its mark. But the Commander didn't know about the tiger tally, and he wasn't stopping to listen.

Ren stumbled forward into the horse's path, dragging Hu with him. "Please, sir, you must listen!" Ren grabbed the horse's bridle. The Commander reached down to shove his son out of the way.

"*I* shot the arrow into the watchtower," Ren said.

"*You* did that?" Commander Zheng suddenly went still. He fixed his son with a terrible stare. "You think this is a game?"

Ren flinched. Hu staggered. "No, sir. It wasn't a game. There really are barbarians out there by the Wall—that's why we did it. Look!"

Ren turned around to show the Commander his back, with the arrows still lodged in his thick coat.

Commander Zheng started. He frowned, but he was listening.

"What more do you need to tell me?" he asked.

"Hu's got half of the tiger," Ren went on.

"He has *what*?" Commander Zheng roared. His hand clenched the handle of his sword.

"Please, sir, don't hurt him! He didn't know!"

Hu reached into the fold of his jacket and took out the half tiger. Ren handed it up to his father.

"Fetch me the Emperor's tally from my study," the Commander told Second Deputy. "Run."

Commander Zheng got down off his horse. He turned the half tiger over. The flames of the torches glinted off its polished surface. Its one eye shone. It snarled. It looked alive.

The deputy came running back, and the Commander put the two pieces of the tiger together. They fitted perfectly. The whole tiger lay in the Commander's hand. All the power of the Emperor crouched there, pent up in its rippled bronze muscles.

Commander Zheng read aloud the characters engraved on the second half. "*Wudi Battalion awaits your orders. Permission to attack. His Imperial Majesty, the Emperor.*"

"Fortune is with us," he said. "Wudi is only two days' march inland. But they can get here in less time than that."

Commander Zheng gave orders sending messengers to the Wall and elsewhere. His words began to flicker and fade away into the shadows. Hu couldn't hear them anymore. There was a roaring in his ears, as if the torches had melded with the fire inside Hu's bones, and the flames were burning through his brain. Hu slithered to the ground in a heap. He vomited at the Commander's feet. Then he blacked out.

REN

"Hu!" Ren bent over the limp body lying on the ground.

"First Deputy!" Commander Zheng ignored the two boys and called up his senior officers. He handed over the second half of the tiger.

"You and Second Deputy take the best horses. Ride hard for Wudi overnight. Tell the Commander there I want his cavalry immediately, plus as many archers as they can mount. Divide the force—Second Deputy leads the cavalry, you the bow contingent. Lie low until you receive my orders, as we discussed earlier. Usual signals. Got that?"

Commander Zheng squatted down. He cast his son a sharp glance as he felt beneath the iron collar for a pulse at Hu's neck. Then he ran his hands down Hu's body and grunted when he found the arrow shaft in his leg.

"Take him to the surgeon," the Commander directed a soldier.

"You—inside," he commanded Ren. "I'll get to the bottom of this later."

Then the Commander rode out into the dark streets.

Ren was feeling extremely tired, and queasy from the sight of Hu being sick. If they all survived beyond the next day, his father might forgive his disobedience. If he was really lucky. If they were all really lucky.

He led the barbarian pony into the stables, now emptied

of all the spare horses. He took the saddle off and had a closer look—she was a bronze-colored mare. Solid and well-groomed.

"Good work," he said, patting her. "There's one less barbarian to invade now that you've left him behind."

"Master Ren! *Aiya!*" It was the cook, standing in the doorway. Fussing as always. "What a night! Swords out, bows drawn—and you here! Good thing Miss Lien is away safe."

Ren's stomach lurched again. Lien was not away safe at all. She was down in the town with Hu's mother and sister, probably feeling alone and frightened.

"You're looking peaked," fussed the cook. "I'll heat you up some broth before you catch a cold."

But Ren had things to do. He still had to go and get his sister. He had to see Hu's family and tell them Hu was injured and Mei's treasure was gone.

"Don't bother," Ren told the cook. "I have to go out again."

"You'll do no such thing." The cook clamped his pudgy hands on Ren's shoulders. "It's more than my life's worth to let you out on a night like this."

"You don't understand," said Ren. "I have to go and find Lien."

The cook studied him.

"I don't believe you," he said. "I'm not such an old numbskull as you think. I may turn a blind eye to a few boyish escapades in peacetime, but I'm not having the wool pulled over my eyes tonight. Now, it's hot broth for you, Young Master."

The cook was no weakling. He steered Ren firmly to the kitchen and dished him out an enormous bowl of soup. He watched Ren eat every mouthful.

"Please, can I go out now?" Ren begged.

"Bed," said the cook decisively, his soft chin wobbling as he shook his head. "And don't try anything, because I'm not taking my eyes off you."

Ren climbed wearily up to his bedroom, followed by the cook. As the cook closed the shutters, Ren caught a glimpse of the familiar view: the hall's tiled roof, the sleeping town, and the silent, ghostly river. He saw nothing moving out there, and he hoped it stayed that way. If the barbarians wanted to take the river route, now that he and Hu had shown it to them, it would take a long time for their army to come down the cliff path single file.

At least his father knew about the barbarians and the tiger tally now. Ren hoped Lien would be all right. He was sure the Lis would try to take care of her, at least.

He unrolled his mattress, curled up in the quilt, and sank into sleep.

Ren dreamed. In his dream he became Archer Yi. He was stalking the sun, with his bow drawn. Just as he let fly, the sun changed. It became a tiger, golden and beautiful. Ren knew he'd shot the wrong thing. But it was too late. The arrow struck the tiger, and the animal changed again. Into Hu. Ren tried to call out, "Where's the tiger? I've got to save the tiger!" But the arrow shot Hu away. Then he was calling for Lien, but a bell was ringing. *Dong. Dong.* The sound drowned out his voice.

Dong. The bronze bell reverberated through the bedroom and shook Ren from his sleep. Ren opened one eye. Gray light came through cracks in the shutters—early morning.

Dong. Dong. The sound was loud, pressing down on him. It came from above—the watch room at the top of the town-hall tower. The warning bell. Beicheng was under attack.

HU

Dong. Dong. Dong. Something was banging through Hu's head. His leg throbbed. He didn't know where he was, but the place smelled. A strange herbal smell that got up his nose and made him dizzy.

The banging stopped.

Hu passed out again.

"We're under fire!" One of those hissing southern voices was shouting nearby. Hu thought he should know the voice, but a rumbling river of noise overwhelmed it. Drums. Hooves. Shouting. Waves of sound pummeled Hu, knocking him in and out of consciousness.

Under fire. It was true. A tongue of fever licked over Hu like a flame. He was burning up. Why had Ma put so much wood in the *kang*? He was being roasted like a goose. Done like a dinner. Where was his mother?

Someone was groaning. Not Hu. Someone else lying next to him.

More people came in, grunting under the weight of a sack. They dumped it down on Hu's other side, and the sack turned into a soldier.

Then more shouting came from outside.

"Company Eleven to the north gate! They've set fire to the north gate!"

Everyone rushed out, leaving Hu between the two strangers. His mind lurched and swayed like a drunk, trying to find a foothold in an unrecognizable world, where everything was burning.

REN

Ren went to see Hu, but he was unconscious and the doctor shooed Ren away. He tried to send a message to Hu's family, but the soldiers in the courtyard refused to leave their post. The only person to pay him any attention was the cook, and by the second day of battle, Ren couldn't stand being near him—he worried and jittered and wouldn't even let Ren open the shutters of his bedroom, for fear of stray arrows. So with the help of a kitchen knife, Ren pried the arrows out of the Li family's armor and put it on again. Then he climbed up to the tower's third story.

The soldiers on watch nodded at him briefly. "Master Zheng." They didn't tell him to go away, or laugh at his old armor. They were tense, like drawn bowstrings. Their eyes flicked over the landscape. One of them twirled the stick for striking the bell between his fingers, around and around.

The top level had windows on all four sides, with no shutters. Ren could see farther from the top level than from his bedroom. What he saw made him shiver. Beicheng was ringed by an army of barbarian horsemen. They were dressed in furs, with strange peaked caps, and they howled like wolves. Waves of them charged in within bowshot and sent volleys of fiery arrows over the town walls, before swirling away again. Ren watched the arrows hiss into the town and sizzle in the snow.

"Good thing we've had this weather," said one soldier. "Or them thatched huts would be cooking by now."

It *was* a good thing, thought Ren. Lien was in one of those thatched huts. He felt a pang of fear for his little sister.

"Will the barbarians go away if they can't get in?" Ren asked.

"Not likely," snorted the soldier. "They've come this far. There's a lot more of them than us. They know we can't hold out for long."

"What about the reinforcements?" Ren said.

"Eh. That's who we're looking for, if ya let us get on with our job."

"Oh."

"Fire at the north gate!" called the soldier at the northern window.

A trail of smoke rose from the gate, a curl of gray against the white fields. Those were the fields where he had first met Hu. There was no escaping out there now.

"Where's the Commander?" the soldier at the north window asked his companions.

"Main gate," said the soldier opposite, pointing.

Ren looked out the south window. He could see the battalion's flag at Beicheng's main entrance. It was red against the white landscape.

"Get him a message," said the first soldier. "Looks like it might be taking hold."

The soldier with the bell stick threw it to his companion and hurtled down the ladder.

"That gate always was rickety. Cheapskate Magistrate!" said the soldier watching the northern side.

The smoke was thickening into black billows. In the courtyard, people were shouting. Ren saw soldiers running through the streets, hugging the walls beneath the eaves to avoid the hail of arrows. He wondered how long it would take the messenger to get to his father.

"No need for a message," said the second soldier. "Reckon he's seen it."

Ren could see the red flag moving toward the smoking gate. He wished his father didn't have to be there. He wished he could be anywhere else. He wished everyone could be anywhere else. Perhaps coming back to Beicheng had been useless. Perhaps he hadn't saved his father or anyone. Perhaps all he'd done was put himself and his sister in danger.

"If that gate goes . . ." said the soldier. He stopped. He didn't have to say anything. Ren knew. If the gate went, so did Beicheng.

The red flag disappeared into the thick smoke.

"Got 'em!" shouted the soldier watching south. "They're here!"

The others rushed over to look. On the far side of the Yellow River, a pinprick of green waved on the bank. A flag. The reinforcements had arrived from Wudi.

One of the soldiers cheered and clapped his comrades on the back.

"Green flag, the Commander said?"

"Eh. Hurry up."

The soldier took a strip of silk out of a box. He attached it to the pulley system by the window and hauled it up the flagpole above them.

The other green flag had stopped at the far side of the river.

"Why aren't they coming any closer?" said Ren. "Don't they realize they have to hurry?"

"Commander's orders," said the soldier. "Time ya got

out of the way, Young Master. Scoot." He jerked his thumb toward the ladder.

Ren could hardly drag his eyes away from the battle all around him. He went down one story to his bedroom, where he disobeyed the cook's instructions and opened the windows wide to watch.

The north gate had disappeared in a haze of smoke. There was no sign of troops on the far side of the river.

In the streets of the town, people were running southward, away from the fire. Soldiers with carts of snow to quench it were trying to push north. Everyone was yelling. Beicheng was in turmoil.

HU

"Hu. Hu!" Someone was calling him. "Hu—wake up. Please! I know you're alive." It was a female voice. Low and cool in his ears like river water.

His leg ached, and he didn't want to move. He was lying under something warm that smelled of horse and fur and— Ren. It was Ren's fur coat. The memory of all that had happened came flooding back. Hu groaned.

"Come on, Tiger. Open your eyes. Don't be a pussycat." It was Mei. She smiled at him. "I found you. In all this mess."

Through the open door, Hu could still hear shouting. He could smell smoke too.

"A fire?" he said.

Mei nodded. "A battle. Drink this." She held a bowl of water to his lips.

"Where am I?"

"In the surgeon's room, in the town hall. The Commander's son left his little sister with us two days ago. For a few hours, he said. When he still didn't come back today, and with the fighting getting worse, Ma thought the little girl should come up here. So I brought her. The soldier on the gate . . . well, it was—you know—him." She looked embarrassed. "Anyway, he let me in and told me you were here."

"Is Ma all right?" Hu asked.

Mei nodded.

"Ah-po?"

"On her knees to the kitchen god, praying."

"Our father?"

"Don't know." They looked around the room full of wounded men. Li San wasn't there.

"Help me out of here," said Hu.

"Of course," said Mei. "I'll look after you." She helped him sit up, put his arms round her neck, and rose steadily to her feet. She was strong. They had borne each other's weight hundreds of times for acrobatic stunts.

"Don't toss me," Hu joked weakly. He was so glad to see her.

Mei carried him across the courtyard to the gate. It was closed. Rat's Teeth and Big Ears were struggling to bar the vibrating gates. A lot of shouting was coming from the other side.

"May I trouble you to let us out?" Mei asked.

The big soldier's ears were going red with effort.

"Please," said Mei, very sweetly.

The wooden beam dropped into place.

"Sorry, miss. You'll be squashed in the rush if we open up. It's a good thing yer here," he added, reaching out to touch her hand. "Yer safer off the streets."

"Big Sister, Big Sister!" A little girl called from the veranda. "Come in! It's dangerous outside, cook says."

Mei turned around. Over her shoulder, Hu saw a little girl. She looked a lot like Ren—but cute.

"Are you my brother's friend?" the girl asked Hu. "Can't you walk?"

"Not anymore," Hu said. It could have been an answer to either question.

"People like us can't come into the homes of people like you," Mei told her. "We'll wait under the eaves."

"I came into your home," Lien answered. "Now you come into mine." She pulled on Mei's arm. She was bossy like Ren too, Hu thought.

Mei carried Hu, following Lien through the hall into the living quarters at the back. At the end of a corridor was a flight of stairs. Mei walked up them slowly, balancing carefully.

"Big Brother!" the little girl called, running into a room at the top of the stairs. "I'm back! I'm back!"

Ren turned around. He swept Lien up in his arms and hugged her tight.

"Ouch," she cried. "Your armor is spiky." Then her eyes grew big as she caught sight of the scene from the window. "Where is our father?" she said.

"There." Ren pointed to a red flag, dipping and waving a short distance from the burning gate.

Lien looked like she might cry. "It's scary," she said. "I want my father to come back."

Ren put an arm around her. Then he saw Mei, and the burden she was carrying. "Hu?" he said uncertainly.

But Hu barely noticed Ren. All that mattered now was what he could see outside: Beicheng was about to be burned down and overrun by howling horsemen.

"That's it!" they heard someone shout in the tower above. Then the bell began to toll insistently.

Hu wondered what that shout meant. Was this it for Beicheng? Had the gate fallen in? The Commander's red flag was moving away from the northern gate now. The bell kept ringing. Was this the end?

"Look!" Mei shouted. "Horses!"

Not more barbarians, thought Hu. His leg was throbbing. He began to shiver with fear.

But Mei wasn't looking toward the wilderness beyond the Great Wall. She was looking south. There, on the far bank of the river, lines of cavalry were drawing up. They began to advance onto the ice at a steady pace.

Chinese troops.

The barbarians surrounding the town had seen them too. They were regrouping. Hordes of men came galloping around from the other side of the town to meet this unexpected threat. More and more of the invaders thundered down the road toward the river.

The Commander's red flag was signaling from Beicheng's main gate now. The bell stopped ringing.

"Don't look," Mei said.

Ren covered Lien's eyes with his hand.

The enemy rushed like the river in flood, straight at the newly arrived troops.

"Where are they all?" muttered Ren. "That's not a full-strength battalion. What happened to them?"

There were way too many of the barbarians, Hu realized. Their sheer numbers would overwhelm the advancing Chinese. Hu felt cold inside. He didn't want to see the armies clash, but his eyes felt as if they were glued open and he couldn't help himself.

The opposing forces were within arrow range of each other now. Horses and men fell on each side. The Chinese reinforcements from Wudi held steady. But in a few minutes they would be smashed by the oncoming charge. Then nothing could stop the barbarians from pouring back into Beicheng through the smoldering hole in its defenses.

"Come on!" said Ren. "Hold the line! Fight!"

The bell began ringing again. *Dong-∂ong-∂ong. Dong-∂ong-∂ong.* In a pattern of three. The reinforcements began to retreat quickly down the frozen river.

"No!" Ren exclaimed.

"They're going?" Hu said. "Have they been beaten already?"

Now the barbarians were at full pelt across the river's icy expanse. In no time at all, they would be on top of the Chinese troops.

Suddenly lines of archers appeared on top of the river cliffs on the far side. The Commander signaled by flag from the walls of Beicheng, and the archers fired.

"The gorge!" said Ren. "They've led the barbarians into the gorge, where they can't escape. Yes!"

The onslaught of horsemen began to waver and crumble under the rain of arrow fire from above.

The bell began ringing again. Beicheng's main gate opened, and the Tiger Battalion charged out.

Most of the barbarian army was caught in the narrow part of the river, between the Wudi cavalry and the Tiger Battalion. From the cliff top, the Wudi archers sent a steady hail of arrows down into the invaders. The trapped barbarians tried to shoot back. But in the tight space and on the slippery ice, they were unable to avoid fallen men and horses, and they began to pile into one another.

The few barbarian horsemen left at Beicheng's north gate galloped toward the river to attack the Tiger Battalion's rear, but the Commander's crossbowmen held them off from the town walls. The other horsemen turned and galloped back up the hill, past Beicheng and over the Great Wall. The two Chinese battalions closed in on what was left of the barbarian army on the river.

"Yes! Yes!" shouted Ren.

"It's nearly over," Mei told Lien. "It's going to be all right."

The invasion had been stopped. Against the odds, Beicheng had survived.

Tears of relief trickled down Mei's face. Hu hugged her. He was crying too.

春

SPRING

REN

Beicheng was safe, but Ren wasn't.

He spent the next two days in his room, trying to keep out of his father's way, hoping there was a vague possibility that his father had forgotten Ren wasn't supposed to be there. The Commander had been very busy since the battle. Maybe Ren would get away with it.

Finally, Commander Zheng sent for him.

The Commander was sitting on the carpet in his study. The two halves of the Emperor's bronze tiger sat before him.

"Come in," he ordered.

Ren went a few steps closer. His father didn't invite him to sit down. Ren stared at the floor. He put his hands behind his back because he couldn't stop them from fidgeting, and straightened up.

"I want the full story," said his father, looking squarely at Ren, with his arms crossed. "Starting with what you were doing outside the Wall, with a convict, in the middle of the night, in possession of the Emperor's stolen property."

Commander Zheng had not forgotten. Ren was miserable. He felt he had nothing to offer in his own defense. He hadn't proved he could be a nobleman, let alone a Commander. He hadn't won the archery competition; instead, he'd shot his only friend. He'd meant to save his little sister, but he'd brought her into a war zone.

"I was looking for Li Hu, sir," Ren mumbled.

"And who gave you permission to do that? Who gave you permission to come back here?"

"No one, sir."

"Since when have you been allowed to do what you please?"

Ren didn't think he was supposed to answer that question. "Sorry, sir," he said.

"Do you know what the consequences are if a soldier is disobedient?" the Commander demanded. "Do you realize that the reason I was sitting here scuffing my boots while those barbarians drew a noose around our necks was because I was waiting for permission to attack? Violating orders is punishable by death."

Ren waited for the wrath of his father, the ancestors, and the Emperor to pour down on him. But the Commander sighed. "As Confucius says, *Control yourself, control your family, control your country*. I have not managed the second part well, it would seem. You will explain what happened outside the town four nights ago."

"I was going to bring Lien here, because of Master Wang. But I needed to find Hu first. I never meant to be out there so late, sir."

"Hmm. So why were you?"

The question turned inside Ren like something bad in his stomach. Shooting Hu had been an accident. A bad dream. Ren fixed his eyes on the floor and twisted the truth.

"It was the barbarians, sir. We ran into them, and they shot at us. Hu got injured. Then we came back as fast as we could. But we couldn't go over the Wall, so we had to go around the long way."

The Commander watched him intently. "Zheng Ren, you gave the password to the guards at the town gate. Do you remember it?"

"Yes, sir. *A nobleman without integrity is like a chariot without an axle.*" Ren was glad to have gotten something right. He wondered how his father knew he'd given the password. From the guards, he supposed. What else did he know?

"How far can a chariot go without an axle?" the Commander asked him. Ren wondered what his father was getting at.

"Nowhere, sir."

"Exactly. Do you know what integrity is?"

"Strength?" Ren guessed.

"Not exactly. Truthfulness and loyalty. No one, not an archer, an officer, or even a Commander, is worth anything without integrity. No matter how slick a shot they might be. Now, you have not told me the truth. Look at me, son."

Ren looked up.

His father frowned. "How did you come by the other half of the tiger?"

"Hu knew where it was." At least that much was the truth and had nothing to do with Ren. He didn't say it had been in the toilet.

"I see." Commander Zheng seemed to be thinking something through.

Ren waited. He suddenly realized, too late, that stealing the Emperor's orders was also likely to be punishable by death—even instant death. And that was just what his father thought Hu had done.

"It wasn't him who stole the tiger. A soldier gave it to his sister," Ren pleaded. "That soldier who escorted Lien and me and Master Wang to Wuzhong."

"Was it, now?" Commander Zheng lifted one eyebrow.

"Yes, sir. It wasn't Li Hu's fault, sir. He didn't know what it was, and I didn't know he had it, until after . . . he got wounded."

"Hmm." The Commander tapped his fingers on a scroll in front of him, then he looked straight at his son. "Zheng Ren, the arrow in Li Hu's leg was one of ours. This battalion's. Not a barbarian one. We've got different barbs, and a maker's mark. Yet no one from the garrison shot at him. How was the boy injured?"

Ren squirmed. "It was me, sir," he whispered.

"Thought so," said the Commander. "By accident?"

Ren nodded.

"So you helped save the town with one shot and ruined someone's life with another," the Commander observed. "How about you tell me where the pony came from too? The one you rode through the town gates."

"I stole it—from the barbarians," Ren mumbled.

"So, my son is a horse thief," said Commander Zheng. His lips twitched at the corners. "As well as disobedient, a liar, and a danger to others."

Ren's heart sank. If the Commander had taken the bronze tiger and hurled it into the river, it couldn't have fallen deeper than Ren's hopes of happiness. Down into centuries of mud and disgrace. Ren felt like a soul on its way to the underworld. He could feel all the gods and ancestors passing judgment on him.

"I will not have disobedience in this family," continued the Commander. "What made you do it, Ren? Why run away and bring your sister into such danger?"

"We found out about Master Wang. He stole the grain with Magistrate Ding—three hundred measures of it. I added up the records in Wuzhong, and then he threatened to sell us."

Commander Zheng looked surprised. "Yes, it *was* three hundred measures. So that's how it is. . . . Why not come to me instead of sneaking off across the Wall?"

Ren's shoulders began to tremble, as well as his hands. His eyes blurred. "Master Wang said I was nobody," he said. "He told me no one cared about the children of a slave girl."

"Did he, now?"

"And you sent me away, so I thought you didn't want me." Ren choked on a sob.

"Sit down," the Commander said to Ren. He put one hand on his son's shaking shoulder. "Listen: your mother was a good woman. I cared about her, even though she was Third Wife and not noble. I brought you and Lien out here because I promised I'd look after you. I sent you both away only to protect you from the barbarians. I care about you too. Do you hear me?"

Ren couldn't say anything, or he would cry.

"You've shown me that you are brave and resourceful, son, but you've got a lot to learn," his father continued. "Now—First Deputy will teach you how to shoot, responsibly. You can keep the barbarian pony, and you can learn about horses from Second Deputy. Got that?" his father said, as if he were giving orders.

Ren nodded. He couldn't stop his welling tears from running down his cheeks. He wanted to throw himself into his father's arms, but the Commander got stiffly to his feet.

"And as for your punishment . . ."

Ren's hopes sagged again.

"I thought of sending you back to the capital, but the danger's over for now, and how could I keep an eye on you there? You've spent the last few days trapped in a town under siege, and that's a lesson in itself. You apologize properly now, and we'll call that punishment enough. This time."

Ren knelt down and touched his forehead to the floor three times in front of his father. "Please forgive my disobedience," he said formally.

Commander Zheng bowed his head slightly. "And the ancestors," he said.

Ren turned and bowed to the ground before the ancestral tablet hanging on the wall. He felt light and dizzy with disbelief.

Only one dark patch still clouded his thoughts. An unhealed wound. He took a breath and braved a question. "Do you know what will happen to Li Hu?" he asked.

"Depends how the leg heals," said his father. "He could end up begging."

Ren shuddered. It was horrible to think of Hu ending up in a gutter. It was horrible to think it was partly Ren's fault. Hu deserved better. Ren knew his father saw Hu as just a poor, dirty peasant, but Ren was determined to make right what he had done, if he could.

"Please—may I ask something from you, sir?" he said.

The Commander lifted an eyebrow, but nodded. Ren explained his idea to his father. The Commander's other eyebrow lifted too. "I'll see," he said. Then he called for a hot bath and waved his son out of the study.

HU

The battle was over, but Beicheng was not the same for Hu and his family. Li San had survived, though, inside the tower on the Wall.

"The soldiers on watch found out the barbarians were there somehow," Mei said. Hu didn't feel like telling her how.

Li San still had three years of hard labor to get through. So did Hu, although he was allowed to stay in town temporarily, while his leg healed enough to walk.

New supplies of grain came into town with the reinforcements, but the Li family had no money to buy any. The bag of turnips was nearly empty. Hu swore his skin was turning purple.

"Better a turnip than a tomb," said Ah-po.

Mei's wedding was off, because Big Ears had been taken in for questioning over the tiger tally. Ma sold the wedding cloth to pay for medicine for Hu. He still couldn't move the foot on his injured leg. It sort of dangled, even when he tried to flex it. The wound still ached as well.

But it wasn't just his leg that bothered Hu. It was the cold nights in the vegetable seller's house, his hungry stomach, and his father away on the Wall. And there was something more, inside him. Every night as he lay in the dark, he remembered all the good times he'd had shooting together with Ren, and their high hopes of winning. Then he remembered the bad stuff: Ren going off to Wuzhong, leaving Hu to face the Magistrate; Ren shooting Hu in the forest. Were poor people really worth less? Hu asked himself. Was it useless to aim for a better life?

Several days after the battle, Magistrate Ding's servant came to the marketplace looking for Ma. Hu's mother didn't want to go to the door. He could tell she was scared it would be more bad news. They couldn't take much more.

"There will be a banquet to celebrate New Year," said the servant officiously, handing her a wooden scroll. "Magistrate Ding has issued orders that your husband be temporarily released from work. The Magistrate requests that you perform again for the Commander and his troops."

Ma bowed. Mei smiled. Hu cheered. His father would be coming back.

"We'll get paid," Mei whispered in his ear.

"We'll get food," Hu whispered back. They laughed.

"The Commander has rescheduled the finals of the archery competition, and Magistrate Ding wants the performance to follow," the servant said.

No! Hu thought. It wasn't fair. He'd made the finals, but he couldn't go in them now because he had no bow.

They could borrow the vegetable seller's old thing for the performance, but it was no good for competition. Besides, he couldn't stand straight by himself yet. His last chance was gone.

Hu helped his mother and sister get everything ready for the performance anyway. They still had the basket of costumes, because there'd been no opportunity to sell them. At least this celebration meant they would have enough money to survive.

Early on New Year's Day, Li San turned up. Ma and Mei were getting dressed and painting their faces.

"Hello, Moon Queen," Li San said, grinning at Ma. "Hello, beautiful daughter. Hello, Tiger." He hugged them all before getting into his costume. "Where's the armor?" he asked.

"Disappeared," said Ma.

"Eh. Well, if that's all we've lost in these bad days, we should thank Heaven, I suppose. I'm so glad you're all here and unhurt."

Mei and Ma looked at Hu and bit their lips, but Li San didn't seem to notice.

"Better get moving," he said. "The tents are already up, and the targets are out in the field. Get dressed, Hu."

"I can't do it just now," Hu said.

"Come on, Tiger, put some teeth into it."

"I can't."

There was silence in the room. Hu unwrapped the rags tied round his leg. Li San saw the bright red scar and the purple bruise, and the foot that still hung at an odd angle. He sucked his breath in sharply and bent down to see the leg. "Devils and demons! How did you do that, kid?"

"It's a long story," said Hu.

"Which he won't tell us," said Mei.

"Does it hurt to wiggle your foot?" Li San asked Hu. He moved it gently in a circle.

Hu shrugged. "Nah. Doesn't hurt as much as it did. But the foot won't do what I tell it. It just flops like a wet noodle."

Li San looked at Ma and Mei. "Why didn't you tell me?" he said.

"We didn't want to worry you," Ma said. "It's hard enough for you up there."

"It'll get better," Hu said. "I'll come and watch today. Next time I'll be right."

Li San put his hands on Hu's shoulders. Hu saw there were tears in his father's eyes. "It won't get that much better, son. With an injury like that, you'll never be able to jump again. Your acrobatic days are over."

A feeling of dizzy unreality came over Hu, the same as it had in front of the Magistrate and later the Commander. This couldn't be true.

Li San gritted his teeth and clenched his fists. "Whoever did this, I'll kill them! Even if it's the Commander himself."

Ma jumped up and grabbed his arm. "No! San-San, don't!" she cried.

"Who did it?" Li San demanded.

"I wish I could tell you everything, but I won't," Hu said unhappily. It wasn't really that he wanted to protect Ren, but he'd seen enough of people being hurt and killed. He wanted to protect his family. He didn't want them to be harmed any more because of him, as they surely would be if Li San took revenge. "You'd only get in more trouble," he said.

Ma kissed Hu's forehead gratefully.

Li San looked sad and beaten, the way he'd looked when they were found guilty by the Magistrate. Hu hated it. He felt like his own heart might break.

"Come on, then," said his father. "We've got a job to do, for better or worse."

He hoisted Hu onto his back, and they set off wearily for the celebrations, with no hopes for a happy New Year.

REN

"Are you ready for the banquet?" the Commander asked, smiling at his children. The sun had come out, and the snowy eaves of the town hall were sparkling.

"Not yet," said Lien, who was having her hair plaited by the cook.

"Yes," said Ren. This time he was allowed to go. He wouldn't miss it for anything.

"Good," said Commander Zheng. He nodded at Ren. "I need your assistance first, with an official matter."

Ren followed his father to one of the offices off the courtyard, pleased that the Commander wanted his help. Could it be something to do with Hu? Ren had been looking forward to the banquet for days, hoping he would see him there.

But it wasn't Hu that Commander Zheng had brought him to see. First and Second Deputy were also in the cold and gloomy office, eyeing a soldier in chains. The soldier's head had been shaved, but Ren knew him instantly by his ears.

"Zheng Ren," said the Commander. "Can you identify this soldier?"

"Yes, sir," said Ren. "He's the one who accompanied me and Lien and Master Wang to Wuzhong, sir."

"And?"

"He's the one that Li Hu's sister got the tiger tally from."

"Thank you. Soldier, the punishment for stealing the Emperor's tally is death."

The big soldier threw himself at the Commander's feet, trembling violently.

"Commander, sir! Spare me! I never knew! Master Wang, he got it from the messenger and said he'd bring it straight to you. Then he told me to throw it in the river and go back to Beicheng. But it was so pretty, sir—I thought it was a waste. I never did it any harm, sir."

"But you didn't bring it to me, did you?" said the Commander severely.

"No, sir," sobbed the soldier. "I didn't know what it was."

Ren was beginning to feel sweaty, despite the cold. He shifted uncomfortably. He had stolen something belonging to the Imperial Army too, but his father had let him off lightly.

"Fortunately for you," said the Commander, "today is Spring Festival. An execution would bring bad luck into the New Year. Officer"—the Commander turned to First Deputy—"please record a sentence of four years hard labor for this soldier. Right—time to go," he said to Ren and Second Deputy.

The four of them waited in the courtyard for horses to be saddled.

"Generous of you to let him off, sir," said First Deputy.

The Commander shrugged. "If you show a man mercy, he'll be twice as loyal." He looked hard at Ren, who kicked the snow with his boot in embarrassment.

"What will happen to Master Wang?" he asked his father. "Will he be executed?"

The Commander frowned. "I'm afraid he's beyond my reach. If I bring this matter up in the capital, it'll be out of my control. Who knows how many heads will roll then? Certainly that soldier's and anyone else who had anything to do with the stolen tally. Better to let him go," he said. Then he mounted his horse and rode out behind the flag bearer.

"Why did Master Wang do it, though?" Ren asked Second Deputy.

"Loathsome creep," answered the officer. "I imagine he planned to escape with his loot while Beicheng burned, and there'd be nobody left to tell the tale. Hurry up on that fine pony of yours, or you'll miss another banquet."

As Ren followed the officers down through the town, he thought about what his father had said: "Anyone else who had anything to do with the stolen tally..." That would mean Hu's sister, and probably Hu too and maybe even, he realized, himself.... Although it seemed terribly unfair that Master Wang and Magistrate Ding would get away with so much, Ren felt a flush of love and thankfulness toward his father.

He scanned the crowd of townspeople around the pavilion, looking for Hu. Ren wondered what would happen to the Lis. Would they still have to wear those iron rings for years and years?

"Big Brother!" Lien was pulling at his sleeve. "Here comes your friend. With his big sister." She bounced up and down and waved at the acrobatic troupe.

Hu was on his father's back. Ren was very happy to see him alive. But when Li San put him down, Ren saw that Hu could only walk by leaning on someone else. He looked very thin, and his skin was sort of yellow.

Ren was about to make his way over to Hu when the drums began to roll for the final round of the archery tournament. First Deputy stood up to call out the list of finalists.

". . . Captain of Company Number Eleven . . . Bowyer Zhang . . . and Beicheng resident Li San."

Why wasn't Hu's name called out? Ren looked to where Hu's family stood. Hu was leaning against his father, explaining something. Of course, Ren remembered, at the Mid-Autumn Festival, they had registered Hu in his father's name. Now Hu couldn't stand straight to shoot, but his father could. Except, they had no bow.

Ren jumped up from the banquet table and dashed out to where his horse was tied up. He had brought his bow today, just in case First Deputy was feeling generous and allowed him to practice on the targets later.

There was a stir through the crowd as Hu's father came to the front, dressed in his performing costume. The iron ring was clearly visible around his neck.

"Under the circumstances," Li San said to First Deputy, "I withdraw."

"Wait!" called Ren, running back. "You can use this."

The Commander raised his eyebrows, but didn't intervene. Ren gave Li San the bow and arrows.

"We'll see if Archer Yi can shoot, shall we?" First Deputy said.

The men lined up.

"Three shots only," yelled First Deputy.

Ren glanced at Hu. He was watching his father intently and singing. Ren knew what the song would be.

Li San flexed the bow to get a feel for it. He fitted an arrow.

Dong! The gong rang for the first shot.

The arrows flew.

Thwack! Bull's-eye for Li San, plus several of the other archers.

Dong! Zing! Thwack! Bull's-eye again.

No wonder Hu could shoot. Li San was good.

The finalists lined up for their last shot.

Dong! There was a rush of air from the bowstrings. *Thwack!* A third bull's-eye for Li San. Yes!

Ren heard the Captain of Company Eleven swear.

"Cursed criminal," snarled the bowyer.

HU

His dad had done it! *One shot to carry his fame to the heavens* . . . But what good was victory to a convicted criminal?

The Commander beckoned the winners over. He presented a horse to the crossbow champion, who bowed repeatedly before he happily led the animal away to show it off to his company. The Li family pushed their way to the front of the crowd to see what Li San would get. Hu noticed there were no more horses being held nearby. He supposed they weren't going to get a prize, because criminals had no rights.

"Congratulations," the Commander said to Hu's father. "Well shot. Unfortunately, I lost my other prize horse in the recent battle. I will award you something else."

The Commander snapped his fingers and a soldier came forward, with a bundle wrapped in red cloth. Whatever it was, it was obviously heavy.

"I trust this humble offering of gold will be useful to you."

Hu gasped. Useful! His family had never seen even a single piece of gold before. They could buy a new house, eat as much as they liked, pay off the taxes. . . .

Li San knelt on the slushy ground before the official table and touched his forehead to the dirt.

"Your skills are wasted on packing mud," Commander Zheng continued. "Kindly make a note of this, Magistrate

Ding . . ." he paused. "With the authority of the Emperor given to me, I declare Li San a free man. You are pardoned."

Hu cheered. He hugged Mei. Ma was radiant.

"I knew this was a good-luck year," said Ah-po.

"Sit down and have a round of wine with us," the Commander said to Li San.

Hu's father bowed again and sat down on the other side of the table from the Commander and Magistrate Ding.

"I understand your son is acquainted with mine." The Commander nodded toward Ren.

Hu stiffened. He didn't want his father to find out it was Ren who had wounded his leg. Mei pulled him as close to the table as she dared, to listen.

Hu's father looked wary and suspicious.

"How old is he?" Commander Zheng asked.

"Born in the year of the Tiger, sir."

"Ah. The same age," the Commander said. "In recognition of your son's services in returning the Emperor's orders, I grant him a pardon too. I would also like to offer him the opportunity of being educated with my son."

Li San's guarded expression changed to surprise. "You do us too much honor, sir. We are poor and lowly people."

"You're not quite so poor now," the Commander said. "No need for such politeness. This is my son's request. He would like to make some compensation for the injury done to your family. Please accept this offer and my family's formal apology."

Hu could see the look of shock on his father's face. Li San knew, now, who was to blame for Hu's disaster. Hu held his breath. Could his father still bring himself to accept a favor from the Commander?

Li San gazed fixedly at the precious prize in red cloth. Then his chin went up. "Thank you, sir. I'll speak to Hu," he said.

Confusion and distrust churned inside Hu. His life had just done another backflip, and he wasn't ready for it. Ren had left his table and was heading toward him. Hu would have walked off if he could, but Mei gave him a gentle push toward the Commander's son.

"Excuse me," said Mei. "I have to get ready for the performance."

Ren caught him. Hu wanted to thump his sister. The Commander's son was the last person Hu wanted to talk to. Just seeing him brought memories rushing back like monsters.

"Will you study with me?" Ren asked eagerly. "You'll have to put up with Confucius and all that, but math isn't so bad. And First Deputy is going to teach us archery."

"Pickle your precious Confucius," Hu muttered. "Why are you doing this? I'm just a useless dirty peasant to you." He looked down uncomfortably at his crooked foot, wrapped in its muddy cloth.

So did Ren. "Hu, I'm sorry," he said. "I mean, I'm sorry I did that. It really was an accident."

Hu groaned.

"Listen!" Ren said passionately. "It doesn't matter if you wear dirty rags and I've got a fur coat. It doesn't matter if one of us is noble and the other's not. You know, what we did that night—warning the tower and everything—we did it together. I couldn't have saved the town on my own. You couldn't have gotten the other half of the tiger to my father without me. Hu, don't you see?" Ren pleaded.

"Nah. I don't know," Hu said. He didn't know what to think. Ren was not the sort to apologize—certainly not to someone like Hu—unless he meant it.

"We're not born in the same year for nothing," Ren went on. He cupped his hands together. "It's like the Emperor's tally. We fit like two halves. You're the other half of the tiger—you're my friend."

"You think?" Hu said. "Doesn't your father know that 'bringing up a tiger is asking for trouble'?" he quoted one of Ah-po's sayings.

"I think he's discovered that," Ren said.

Hu saw he had a choice to make. He knew now that the world was a harsh place. The year of the Tiger had scarred him forever. He had set out to make things better for himself and his family, but being around Ren had destroyed so much of his life. Some of it, like his leg, money could not buy back.

But he didn't have to give up. In the end he *had* helped save his town and won a better life for his family, even though it had cost him a lot. And it *had* been with Ren's help.

Hu thought too of the beautiful characters dancing across the tiger tally's back. He would like to be able to read and write those. He looked at the still-icy river, a silvery path winding into the future. A different future from anything he'd imagined. No more acrobatics, but maybe something good in a different way. Hope fluttered in him again, like one of the battalion's banners.

"Let's have something to eat," Ren said. "The next course has arrived."

"Doesn't smell like turnips," Hu said. "People like me don't eat at banquets."

"Turnips are for horses," Ren said. "And you're my guest now."

"Then I propose a toast," said Hu with a grin. It felt like it had been forever since he'd smiled. "To the year of the Tiger! The year Zheng Ren learned who's Hu."

This time it was Ren who smiled.

"Long live the Tigers," he said.

EPILOGUE
The Second Half of the Tiger Returns

To His Imperial Majesty,
Ruler of the Han Kingdom,

I have the honor to report: barbarian forces
numbering over ten thousand were defeated at
Beicheng on the twentieth day of the twelfth month.

Repairs to the Great Wall are almost complete.
I hereby return the Imperial tally. The battalion
awaits your further instruction.

May the blessing of Heaven go with
Your Majesty in the New Year.

Your loyal servant,
Commander Zheng
Beicheng

HISTORICAL NOTE

The people and events in *Year of the Tiger* are invented. So is the town of Beicheng. But something like this could have happened. At the time this story is set, in the second century AD, China had an empire as rich and powerful as Rome's. The Han Emperors who ruled it had large armies and a complicated system of government.

The Great Wall was first built three hundred years before the time of this story. Its purpose was to defend China against tribes living on the Mongolian plains to the north and in the deserts to the west. In western China much of the Wall was built from pounded earth. It was wide enough on top for three horsemen to ride together.

In Imperial China, distances were measured with a unit called *li*. The English word "miles" is used in this book to mean *li*. One *li* equals half a kilometer.

The Chinese year traditionally begins with the Spring Festival. (This is usually called "Chinese New Year" in English.) Spring Festival happens sometime in January or February, when the moon is "black," or barely visible. Each year is given the name of an animal: Rat, Ox, Tiger, Rabbit, Dragon, Snake, Horse, Sheep, Monkey, Rooster, Dog, or Pig. These names go around in a twelve-year cycle. So if you are born in one year of the Tiger (e.g., 1998), you turn twelve in the next year of the Tiger, and so on.

ALISON LLOYD lived in China for two years. She loves history — both the big sweep of events and the little details of how people lived. She says her favorite stories are about people's deep feelings: "hope and despair, loyalty and betrayal, love and loss." That's why she wrote *Year of the Tiger,* her first novel.